A loud bo

Olivia grabbed her plane seat. "What was that?"

Flames burst from the plane front. Smoke poured over the windshield.

Caleb shifted his headset microphone. "Mayday. Mayday."

"Caleb, what's going on?"

"Someone's trying to shoot us down. I can land this if I can find an open field, but in this section of the forest, that's not likely."

Panic seized her. "So what can we do?"

"I know you can't remember anything, but do you think you've ever gone skydiving?"

Olivia lurched upright. "What? You've got to be kidding me."

He glanced at her. "I guess that's a no? My K-9, Ranger, is trained to skydive with me, but I don't have time to give you a lesson—and I can't tandem dive with you both."

The ground rushed up at them. "Please, tell me there's a plan B."

"There sure is." Caleb's bluish-green eyes were alight. "Hold on..."

Deena Alexander grew up in a small town on the south shore of eastern Long Island, where she met and married her high school sweetheart. She recently relocated to Florida with her husband, three kids, son-in-law and four dogs. Now she enjoys long walks in nature all year long, despite the occasional alligator or snake she sometimes encounters. Deena's love for writing developed when her youngest son was born and didn't sleep through the night.

Books by Deena Alexander

Love Inspired Suspense

Crime Scene Connection
Shielding the Tiny Target
Kidnapped in the Woods
Christmas in the Crosshairs
Hunted for the Holidays
Hiding the Witness
Exposing Lethal Secrets

Visit the Author Profile page at LoveInspired.com.

EXPOSING LETHAL SECRETS

DEENA ALEXANDER

LOVE INSPIRED SUSPENSE
INSPIRATIONAL ROMANCE

LOVE INSPIRED® SUSPENSE
INSPIRATIONAL ROMANCE

Recycling programs for this product may not exist in your area.

ISBN-13: 978-1-335-98068-7

Exposing Lethal Secrets

Love Inspired
22 Adelaide St. West, 41st Floor
Toronto, Ontario M5H 4E3, Canada
www.LoveInspired.com

Printed in Lithuania

MIX
Paper | Supporting responsible forestry
FSC® C021394

Glory ye in his holy name:
let the heart of them rejoice that seek the Lord.
—*Psalms* 105:3

Mikki—your strength and courage astound me

ONE

"Getting out late today, huh, Olivia?" Marty Jenkins, an older gentleman Olivia Delaney had worked with for the past five years, tipped his trademark tweed Scally cap as he passed her.

Friend or foe? No way to tell, so Olivia forced a smile and hooked a thumb toward the exit. "Just grabbing something I forgot, then I'm on my way out."

"Well, you have a good weekend."

"You, too." A shiver raced up her spine as they passed each other in the long corridor. Must be the air conditioning, kept cooler than was comfortable in deference to all the computers in her late father's office building. At least, that was what she told herself. She resisted the urge to turn and look over her shoulder—barely. If someone was watching, no way did she want to alert them to her intentions. She continued at her casual pace, heels clicking like gunshots against the tile floors.

When she reached her supervisor's office, where she'd conveniently "forgotten" her bag when she met with him earlier, she glanced discreetly down the corridor behind her, then let herself in. Holding her breath, she hurried across the room and inserted a flash drive she'd prepared into the computer. She'd downloaded most of the proof she needed that someone was running a money-laundering operation through her father's investment firm. She needed just a few more files, and then she just had to make sure that evidence stayed put until she could dig through it all, determine who exactly was involved and alert the authorities.

Sweat trickled down her back, and the seconds ticked by loudly in her head, prodding her to move faster lest she get caught locking the company's files and access to their bank accounts.

With a sigh of relief, she completed her task, yanked the flash drive from the computer and tucked it into her skirt pocket for safekeeping. That specific flash drive had an encryption key for unlocking the files and accounts. Without it being physically inserted into a company computer, no one would be able to access those files.

No way would she allow whoever was using her father's investment firm as a front for a money-laundering scheme to get away with it.

Now, if she could just make her way out of there before anyone realized what she'd done. She'd waited to lock everything up until the building was mostly empty of her coworkers—people she was friendly with, had socialized with, people she knew...

At least, she'd thought she did, before she came across a journal tucked away in a locked box in her father's closet when she'd been cleaning out his home. Her brother, Tristan, hadn't let her anywhere near their father's office, but he'd left the rest of the house to Olivia to deal with.

Well, half brother. Olivia had two half siblings, Tristan and Amy. They'd had no interest in their father on a personal level, and now they could let that show. Tristan and Amy's mother had walked out a long time ago, leaving them to be raised by a man who, according to them, hadn't wanted to be a father. They claimed he was a ruthless tyrant who didn't care about anything other than his business.

Olivia's experience with him had been so much different, and a point of contention between her and Tristan for as long as she could remember. As if it were her fault he'd found God after marrying Olivia's mother. She couldn't help it, nor would she apologize for the fact that she and her dad had been very close, especially after her mother passed away when Olivia was a teenager.

So she'd applied herself to honoring his memory as she cleaned out the house. Then she'd found that safe. Grief and guilt had nearly overwhelmed her when the combination to the lock turned out to be her own birthday.

The journal contained information that didn't make sense—shell corporations, questionable real estate transactions and large amounts of cash being moved around—in addition to instructions and passwords to access files on a laptop hidden with the journal. Apparently, her father had stumbled across a massive money-laundering scheme.

Unfortunately, with Tristan having majority control of the company, her dad had needed proof of who was involved before he would risk moving to take them down. Was it a coincidence he'd died of a heart attack before he was able to determine that answer?

Olivia had discussed the situation with Amy, who had inherited a portion of the firm along with Olivia and Tristan. Tristan might be in charge, but Amy was an active owner, too, more so than Olivia. After all, Amy had graduated college ten years ahead of her and gone straight to work for their father. Olivia had a good relationship with Amy and thought her sister could help. But Amy had dismissed her concerns as paranoia.

Still, Olivia couldn't let it go, especially when she began to notice shadows lingering outside her house late at night, and she became prone to sudden attacks of goose bumps that raised the hairs on the back of her neck while she was going about her daily routine—like now, even if her current mission could never be called routine.

There was no way Olivia would let the reputation her father had worked so hard for go up in flames because Tristan was a greedy—

She shook off the thoughts as she hooked her canvas tote over her shoulder and hightailed it out of the office.

She never should have stayed in California. She'd been planning to go back to her home in Florida after attending her father's service and dealing with his belongings, but she'd felt so guilty about his death, about not being there for him.

And so she'd decided to take a position with Delaney Investments a little more than a year ago. Tristan had been quick to point out that while her degree might have been in business, she had no experience since she'd decided to pursue a career in art. He'd offered her an entry-level position as an analyst, take it or leave it. He and Amy were twelve and ten years older than her, and they'd both started as analysts, after all. Olivia could work her way up to a leadership role, just as they'd done.

The job hadn't helped her feel closer to her father, though. She ignored the dull ache in her chest she'd grown used to this past year—the guilt over leaving her father and sister, the pain of his passing, the desperate urge to return to Florida and the life she'd made for herself there—as far away as she could get from Tristan.

None of it mattered now. Forgoing the elevator, she pushed through the door to the stairway and hurried down the three flights to the lobby, her footsteps echoing in a steady rhythm she dared not increase. She was almost out. A few more minutes, and she'd be home free.

Please, God, let me make it out of here without anyone stopping me and asking questions I can't answer.

As soon as she checked the files she'd downloaded, she'd get the flash drive to the FBI and wash her hands of the whole situation. If Tristan was involved in illegal activities, which she suspected he was, she would see him in jail. Amy could decide what to do with Delaney Investments, keep it, run it, sell it—Olivia didn't care, as long as she could walk away. She'd honored her father, had tried to make a life here, had even gotten engaged, for all the good it had done her. Then again, what was one more betrayal?

When she reached the bottom of the stairway, she shoved the door to the lobby open and breathed a sigh of relief that was cut short when alarms started to shriek. An announcement blared over the loudspeakers, initiating lockdown procedures.

Oh, no! Ten seconds. She had ten seconds to get out before the front doors locked, and she'd be stuck in the building and at Tristan's, or whoever's, mercy. She full-out sprinted for the door, despite the high-heeled pumps she wore, and managed to nip through without breaking an ankle just before the locks clicked into place. Without slowing, she barreled down the front steps and crossed the courtyard.

A gunshot tore through the late afternoon crowd from

somewhere behind her. She wrapped her arms over her head and kept running as the shot hit a display window, shattering the glass. Pedestrians screamed and ran, some trying to flee, most diving behind the nearest cover they could find. Olivia kept running, tears streaming down her cheeks, breath coming in shallow gasps. When she reached her limo, she dove through the door her driver held open to the back seat, keeping her head low.

He slammed the door shut behind her, rounded the limo and jumped in. "Where to?"

They'd shot at her? Seriously? No way would her brother have ordered that. But what were the chances it was just a random, unrelated shooting at the exact moment she was attempting to flee the building with sensitive information that would likely put someone behind bars? Slim to none.

She turned to peer out the back window at the bedlam unfolding as Larry rocketed away from the curb. They'd actually shot at her on a crowded street with absolutely no regard for collateral damage. What had she stumbled upon? Was it more than she suspected, or were these people really so greedy they'd risk killing innocent people to stop her from outing them? Of course, she had cut off access to their money. *Oh, God, please don't let anyone be injured...or worse.*

She didn't dare take the time to sort through the information she'd downloaded. Nor would she waste time trying to find someone at the FBI to listen to her concerns as she'd initially planned. No, the local police could have it all and make whatever sense they could of it, and she was out of here. Once Larry rounded the corner and she could no longer witness the scene, she turned back around, secured her seat belt and laid her head against the back of the seat. "Take me to the nearest police station, please, Larry."

"Yes, ma'am." He didn't ask her what happened, didn't inquire if she was okay, simply did as she asked. When his cell phone rang, he answered quietly.

Olivia missed driving, missed the freedom of losing herself on a highway or a winding back road where no one else knew where she was and she could spend hours just blasting the radio and admiring the scenery. She missed long walks in the swampy forest with nothing but the sounds of nature for company. California might be where she was born and raised, but Florida was home. And whatever happened next, as soon as she handed this information off, she was going home.

She squeezed her eyes closed, tears still leaking, and worked to steady her breathing. Her heart pounded painfully against her ribs. Her feet were killing her, thanks to being forced to flee in the stupid pumps she'd kept on so as not to draw suspicion. She toed them off, easing the ache in her arches.

She set her bag on the seat beside her and dug through for her cell phone. When she found it amid the clutter, she pulled it out, then simply sat, clutching it in her hands and staring.

Who could she call? The only friends she'd made since returning to California worked for the company, and she had no idea who she could trust. Too many of the players her father had uncovered had connections to Tristan. At best, her brother was involved. At worst, he was the mastermind. Her ex-fiancé was just as corrupt and loyal to Tristan, so he was out. And she couldn't call Amy and get her mixed up in this mess.

So, who could she turn to for help? No one. Giving up, she tossed the phone back into the bag with a little more force than necessary.

She worked to calm herself, closing her eyes and visualizing a trail through palm trees and moss-covered oaks, imagining she could hear the birds chirping, even the bellow of a gator—from a safe distance, at least. The sounds of the city faded, her heart rate began to slow, and the soft hum of the tires against pavement began to soothe her.

When she noticed the gradual but increasing incline, the twists and turns indicating they were leaving the city, she opened her eyes. Confused, she frowned at Larry in the rearview mirror. "Where are we going?"

Without a word, Larry handed her an unmarked, sealed envelope over his shoulder.

She took it, slit it open with one long, salmon-colored nail and glanced inside, then pulled out a photo of her sister, her gaze shooting once again to Larry. Larry, who had been hired by her brother, who Tristan insisted drive her everywhere. "What's going on here?"

"I need you to hand over the flash drive, and everyone will forget about the information you stole from the company."

"What?" She shook her head, trying to clear the haze of betrayal—again—which seemed to be a recurring theme throughout her life. "What are you talking about? I didn't *steal* anything."

And technically, she hadn't, considering she owned a portion of the company. Tristan would have been happy if she'd stayed in Florida as a silent partner and just collected her substantial profits once a month, but even if she had, she should still have access to any information moving through the firm should she wish to review it.

Larry glared back at her in the rearview mirror as he navigated the winding mountain road. "Let's not split hairs, Olivia. Just hand over whatever you took, and I'll drop you at the airport. You can go on back to Florida and resume whatever life you abandoned to come out here."

"I'm not giving you anything, and you can just pull over right here and let me out." She folded the photo and stuffed it into her skirt pocket next to the flash drive, then let the envelope drop as she scooted as far toward the passenger side door as the seat belt would allow, intent on diving out the minute he stopped. Then she looked out at the rugged mountain terrain on her left, and the sheer drop-off into the desert on her right. Not that she knew where she was or how she'd get back to civilization, but she was done playing games with Larry.

When Larry didn't even slow down, she returned her gaze to him and found herself staring down the muzzle of a handgun he'd aimed over his shoulder at her.

A vise squeezed her chest, forcing all the air from her lungs. She tried to wheeze out a response but couldn't force the words past the lump of fear in her throat. Jumping out would do her no good. She'd either fall to her death down a cliff, or he'd easily shoot her as she tried to cross the road and flee up the mountainside.

Without warning, she grabbed his wrist, catching him off guard, and tried to wrestle the weapon from him.

His hold on the gun loosened for a moment, but then he recovered.

Olivia jammed her hand into her canvas bag, feeling around in it as she gripped his wrist. She forced the weapon against the passenger headrest to keep him from getting a clear shot at her.

He fought against her hold while still trying to keep the car on the road, swerving wildly across both lanes, and fired. The back passenger window shattered.

The instant she felt the pepper spray canister in her bag, she yanked it out, aimed it at him and let loose a short stream right in his face. She squinted her eyes, tears blurring her vision. Probably not the smartest move while he was driving and she was in the vehicle, but desperate times and all that.

He screamed something incoherent and finally released his hold on the gun, dropping it to the floor in front of her. The limo careened toward the narrow shoulder.

Olivia tried to lunge over the seat to grab the wheel, but her seat belt yanked her back.

Rubbing his eyes with one large hand, Larry missed the hairpin turn, sending the limo plunging off the road and over the cliff side.

All sense of time and direction distorted as they bounced and tumbled down the embankment. Her screams mixed with Larry's until there was nothing but an all-encompassing roar that threatened to deafen her.

Something slammed against her head. Her vision tunneled, a tidal wave of black crashing in from both sides. Pinpricks of light danced in front of her eyes, and she began to pray even as she lost her battle with consciousness.

Her eyelids fluttered, the world around her nothing but a blur. The overpowering odor of gasoline yanked her awake, and the smell of smoke followed right on its heels.

The crackle of flames reached her before she could force her eyes all the way open, and she had to wait a moment for her vision to clear.

Pain threatened to split her head when she tried to lift it from the seat. Nausea surged, sending bile rushing up her throat. A feeling of intense terror washed over her, and she sat perfectly still, forcing air in and out, the acrid stench burning her lungs. Wherever she was, she had to get out of there. Now.

She looked around, trying to catalogue as many details as possible. She was in a wrecked car. A man lay half in, half out of the vehicle, having gone through the windshield. She unbuckled her seatbelt and inched forward slowly, then reached for his wrist, felt for a pulse—too late.

Who was he? Did she know him? Did she love him?

She studied his form. Nothing. There was nothing at all familiar about him. The overwhelming sense of fear didn't abate—if anything, it increased the longer she studied him. But there was no time to contemplate that now.

Thankfully, there was room enough for her to wriggle past him and out. She landed hard on her side in the sand, then scrambled backward away from the vehicle. Or rather, the mangled remains of what appeared to have once been a limo. But why had she been riding in a limo? She choked back the fear, had to or it would paralyze her. Her mind was an absolute blank. She had no memory of what had happened to make her so frightened, what she was doing in a limo or where she'd been going. She couldn't even recall her own name.

She blinked a few times in rapid succession, trying to clear the horrible burning from her eyes, then crab walked farther back from the burning vehicle. She had to stay calm.

A glint caught her attention, and she saw a handgun lying on the ground a few feet from the car. Did she own a gun? She had no idea. But with the intensity of the fear threating to consume her, she wasn't taking any chances. And she wasn't about to leave a weapon lying in the desert where some kid might come across it and get hurt.

She stood, her bare feet burning in desert sand made even hotter by the fire, waited out a wave of dizziness, then grabbed the weapon and stuffed it into the waistband of her skirt, snug against her back. It was then that she noticed the blood soaking the front of her lightweight, ivory linen jacket and silk blouse. Hers?

It didn't seem to be. She must have gotten it on her when she checked the man's pulse. She gingerly removed the jacket and dropped it on the ground, then untucked her ivory blouse and let it fall over her skirt, hoping it would conceal the weapon.

She surveyed her surroundings and managed to find two black pumps she assumed were hers. It would be ridiculous to try to escape wearing pumps, but probably more so to attempt it barefoot on the blistering sand. Since there didn't seem to be any way for her to climb back up the sheer mountainside they'd apparently gone over, she simply stepped into her shoes, turned toward the desert and started walking.

The desert sun beat hard on Caleb Miller. He paused to admire the lake shimmering in the distance, even knowing it was nothing more than a mirage—like so many beautiful but dangerous things. Savoring the view, he moved to a cropping of boulders, checked for rattlesnakes and scorpions, then leaned his back against the largest of the rocks, sending a couple of annoyed lizards skittering away. "No reason to run, guys. I'd have shared."

Ranger, his long-haired German shepherd, barked once, then moved into the shadows beside him. Given that the fur on Ranger's head, face and back was mostly black, with the lighter tan and rust colors running along his belly and legs, Caleb had to be careful with him in the hot sun. But Ranger was used to the desert, and he enjoyed the outdoors, reveled in the peace and quiet the two of them found when they took a break from work.

Caleb set his wide-brimmed hat aside on the boulder, shifted his sunglasses to the top of his head, then closed his eyes and tilted his face up to the sun for just a moment. They'd needed this break. The case he'd just closed with Jameson Investigations, where he worked as an agent with his K-9 partner, had been difficult and had left them both drained. They needed time to reset, recuperate and recharge.

A week ought to do it, and then he might think about taking another mission. Hopefully, one with a better outcome, where he could once again move toward his goal of saving as many lives as possible to make up for too many lost. He offered another quick prayer for the victims they hadn't been able to save, as he did every time he thought of them.

Or maybe he'd disappear longer this time, once again seek that elusive forgiveness everyone assured him would help him heal. Who knew? For today, he just needed the solitude and tranquility only nature could offer. They'd only arrived in the California desert that morning, and already the anxiety had begun to abate. This time, he'd been able to keep his eyes closed for almost a full minute before visions better left in the past intruded.

Ranger whimpered and nudged his head against Caleb's hip.

"Sorry, boy. You're right, as usual. What would I do without you to remind me of what's important?" Caleb straightened and shrugged off his backpack, and his thoughts, then propped the bag on the boulder beside his hat and dug through for Ranger's water bottle. He filled the bowl attachment and held it out so Ranger could drink his fill before closing it up and taking a few slugs from his own bottle. "You want to chill here for a while, boy?"

Ranger tilted his head and studied him.

"All righty. Sounds like a plan then. We'll hang out here for a bit and watch the sunset, then go back to the RV and have some dinner." Tai chi in the desert at sunset sounded like just what he needed. His boss, Zac Jameson, often suggested meditation, but Caleb never had been able to find peace in sitting still. As he returned his attention to the backpack to pull out the white mat he always carried for Ranger to lie on, movement in his peripheral vision snagged his attention. A plume of smoke billowed fairly close by, intruding amongst the wispy white clouds dotting the cerulean sky.

He stilled, tilted his head, listened. Nothing. No screams, no sirens, no calls over the police scanner he carried on his belt.

He wanted to ignore it, wanted to pretend he hadn't seen it, wished fervently he could close his eyes, open them again, and it would be gone. But he tried, and it didn't work. The smoke still poured from something then got caught up by the warm, dry winds that would fan those flames far too quickly. With a sigh, he left the mat where it was, stuffed both water bottles back into the backpack beside it, and checked Ranger's booties were secure. "Come on, boy."

He stood, then paused. Run back to the RV for the fire extinguishers, or head straight to the fire and hope someone had called it in, then do so if it seemed no one had? Even in the late afternoon heat, he could jog the mile to the RV in under ten minutes, then another ten back. No. It was too long to wait. He'd check out what was burning then decide what, if anything, to do. Surely, someone had noticed the smoke visible from miles away and called it in. Even along this desolate stretch of mountains and desert, tourists and campers occasionally meandered through.

He shouldered the backpack, slapped his hat and sunglasses back on, then started off at a jog.

Even without the command to search, Ranger slipped easily into work mode, keeping pace at his side, as he would until Caleb issued further commands.

Go figure. He'd chosen the most remote location he could think of to go off grid for a while, and what happens? A fire that could spread quickly, fueled by dry grasses and scrub. Rachel had always said if it weren't for bad luck—

He slammed the door mid-thought. What Rachel did or didn't say no longer mattered. It hadn't since the day she'd divorced him to marry someone else, breaking his heart, destroying him, and shattering all his dreams for the future. Well, technically, that wasn't true. His dreams weren't shattered, it was just that someone else was living them, someone who was supposed to have been his best friend, someone he'd trusted. That had been his biggest mistake. If you didn't trust anyone, kept everyone at arm's length, then you couldn't get hurt. A philosophy he embraced fully after Rachel had walked out.

And, besides all of that, he didn't believe in luck. Somewhere along his journey toward trying to heal, in one of the many isolated locations he'd chosen to disappear into, he'd discovered that the only place he could fully put his trust was in God. People, no matter how well-intentioned they might seem, always betrayed you in the long run.

The odor of smoke increased the closer he got to the point of origin. He paused, fished a bandanna out of his backpack, soaked it with water from his water bottle and tied it around his face. "Stay, Ranger. I'll only be a minute."

A quick scan of the deserted area assured him Ranger should be okay for a couple of minutes while he approached the burning vehicle lying in a heap at the bottom of a cliff. He looked up, but without equipment, no one could have made the climb back to the road. And there was no sign of emergency vehicles. He rounded the car, fully engulfed in flames, and knew he was too late to save anyone who had been trapped inside. "God, please let everyone have gotten out."

As he reached the far side, a set of footprints in the soft sand leading away from the vehicle gave him hope his prayer might have been answered. He started to follow the trail, then whistled for Ranger as soon as he was far enough from the flames that his partner wouldn't be in danger.

While he waited, he pulled his sat phone out of his pocket and dialed the first number programmed in.

Zac Jameson answered on the first ring. "I thought you were lying low for a while."

"Yeah, well, so did I, but it seems I have a problem."

"What do you need?"

Okay, so there *was* one person Caleb could trust. Zac Jameson, head of Jameson Investigations, was the single most trustworthy person Caleb had ever met. But he was the exception, not the rule. Zac had started Jameson Investigations years ago, after his own tragedy struck. He'd been tracking down and hiring agents ever since. Now, he commanded a wide network of agents and offered all kinds of services, from bodyguards to search-and-rescue teams, anywhere in the country. "Can you track where my phone is right now and send emergency vehicles? I have a single car accident. The car is fully on fire, but even though it's surrounded by mostly sand, a slight change in wind direction toward the scrub and brush, and we'll be dealing with an entirely different situation."

"Are you and Ranger okay?"

"What?" He scanned the area to be sure he hadn't missed a second vehicle. "Oh, right. No. I mean, yeah. Sorry. We're fine. It wasn't my car. I just came upon it while we were hiking in the desert."

"Sit tight. Angela's already on it."

While Zac might be the most trustworthy person he knew, Angela Ryan was the most efficient. The woman was Zac's right hand and a multitasking genius.

"Are you going to wait with the vehicle?" Zac asked.

"No. There's a set of footprints leading away from the car. I'm going to follow them and make sure no one needs help."

"All right, but be careful and keep me in the loop."

"Sure thing, boss. And thanks." Caleb disconnected the call and stuffed the phone back in his pocket, then took a moment to put Ranger's vest on so he understood they were no longer in vacation mode.

Ranger lowered his head, clearly needing more time off than they'd been allowed.

Caleb ruffled his fur. "It's okay, boy. As soon as we find whoever's wandering around out there, we'll return to our time off. I promise."

But what could he use for Ranger to scent? Not that Caleb couldn't simply follow the footprints, he could, for now, but one strong wind, or one spot where the sand hardened, and he would lose the trail, then lose precious time trying to backtrack and pick it back up again. And, while Ranger could search without an item, it would make it faster and easier if he had one. An increasing level of anxiety warned he might be running out of time.

He glanced around the scene, searching for anything the victim might have dropped or left behind, a wallet, a purse, a hat, a shoe… Not only for Ranger, but in case they could ID any victims. Then he spotted a discarded off-white jacket. He lifted it by the collar and noticed the bloodstains covering the front. His sense of urgency ratcheted up. If whoever was wandering the desert was injured and unused to the intense heat, they could get into trouble real fast. He held the jacket out for Ranger, then issued the search command.

Ranger sniffed a few times, then took off along the footprint trail with Caleb close behind. It wasn't long before Ranger barked and shot ahead.

"Hold!"

Ranger stopped short and looked back at him.

Not that Ranger would ever hurt anyone, but the last thing a disoriented, frightened accident victim needed was a nearly one-hundred-pound dog barreling toward them in the middle of the desert, even if he did have the best of intentions.

Caleb jogged to catch up. "Heel."

Ranger fell instantly in step at his heel as they continued forward.

Caleb skirted a group of boulders and found a woman with long blond hair tangled around her shoulders crouched behind a cactus, aiming a 9mm straight at his chest.

"Whoa! Hey!" He threw his hands in the air. "Stop!" He issued the command harsher than necessary, and Ranger froze mid-step at his side. "Ma'am, I—"

"Don't you move. Not one muscle, or I will shoot." While her hands, both clutching the weapon, shook wildly, the look in her eyes left no doubt she'd follow through on the threat.

TWO

"Back away." The last thing she wanted was to have to shoot anyone, *if* she even knew how to fire the weapon, which she wasn't sure she did. But she had no idea who the stranger standing in front of her with his hands over his head was. Or who she was, for that matter. "Please. Just go. Leave me alone."

"Ma'am. I'm not trying to hurt you. I found a car in flames at the bottom of a cliff, and Ranger tracked you here."

"Ranger?"

"My K-9 partner. My name is Caleb Miller. I'm an agent with a company called Jameson Investigations, and this…" He nodded toward the beautiful black-and-rust dog at his side. "Is Ranger. We're here to help you."

"Why?" She struggled to remember if she'd ever seen him before. But her mind was a total blank, as if someone had wiped all of her memory circuits, leaving only the unrelenting certainty that she was in mortal danger. From him? She struggled to hold the weapon steady. It didn't feel familiar in her hand. Could it have been hers? Or did it belong to the man she left behind in the car? That seemed more likely. Had he kidnapped her?

Caleb frowned. "Ma'am, are you all right?"

"I don't know." She hadn't meant to let that slip, but it was the truth, so she just let it hang between them.

He tapped a couple of fingers against his temple. "You have a head injury, ma'am. Will you let me at least check it for you?"

A sob sneaked out, and pain radiated through her chest. Fear? Broken ribs from the crash? Or was she on the verge of a heart attack?

"May I please come closer?" Without waiting for a response, he took one step forward.

"No." She lifted the weapon, firmed her grip. Was the gun even loaded? How long would it take him to figure out she had no clue how to use it? "Do not move."

The dog growled low in his throat, clearly responding to his handler's distress. Or maybe hers.

"It's okay, boy." Caleb laid a gentle hand on Ranger's head without shifting his gaze from her. "Okay. How about this? I'll kneel down right here beside Ranger, and you lower the weapon. Then, we'll talk."

She studied him, wrestled with the decision of whether or not to trust him, but she couldn't seem to bring herself to do so. Had trust ever come easy to her? Or was it just because of the amnesia? Too many questions battered her. She'd be relieved if she could answer even one. At least then she might not feel so lost and alone.

He slowly took off his hat, ran a hand over his dark-colored buzz cut and set the hat upside down on the sand beside him. The sunglasses followed, and he dropped them in the hat. Did he think seeing his friendly hazel eyes would distract her? Make her trust him? "If it's okay to reach into my back pocket for my wallet, I can show you my ID and a Jameson Investigations business card."

When he started to reach behind him, panic assailed her. "No! Don't move. I mean it. Please, don't make me shoot you."

"No, no. Hey. It's okay. There's no need for any shooting." He held his hands out in front of him as if trying to ward off whatever bullets she might fire. "It's all right. How about if we just sit here for a few minutes and talk?"

But her focus had shifted past him to something shimmering in the distance. As she watched, a gleaming black blur split into two, both moving toward them at a brisk pace.

Caleb glanced over his shoulder, clearly not expecting to see anything since his attention snapped right back to her, then did a double take. "Look, ma'am, whatever's going on here, you'd better tell me right now, because two men in suits are running toward us, neither of whom is carrying any rescue equipment. I don't want you to shoot me in the back if I have to pull the weapon holstered at my side to deal with them."

Heat scorched her face; her heart rate shot through the roof. Were those men coming for her?

Caleb's attention ping-ponged back and forth between her and the men moving toward them, but his voice remained perfectly calm, as if he had all the time in the world to chitchat. "Can you at least tell me your name?"

Before she could answer, one of the men moving toward them swung a very scary-looking weapon into view. "Olivia! Stay right where you are!"

She shifted the gun, aiming it past Caleb at the two intruders.

"Olivia? Is that your name?" Caleb asked, lowering his hands to his sides.

Was it? Maybe, but it brought no spark of recognition. She wanted to scream, needed a minute to collect her thoughts. This was all happening too fast. "I don't know!"

"Okay. Don't panic." Caleb inched closer. "From the looks of it, you have a pretty serious head wound."

Frowning, unaware she'd been injured before he pointed it out, Olivia reached up one hand and pressed her fingers to the side of her head Caleb indicated. They came away bloody. Was it her own blood soaking her blouse and jacket?

"It's perfectly normal that you might not remember some things, especially the time period directly before the accident." He took another step.

"It's not some things. It's everything. I can't even remember my own name. My mind is like a vacuum," she sobbed, frantic to be anywhere but where she was. Her hands shook harder, one of them now slicked with blood. She was going to drop the gun. Not that it mattered. She clearly wasn't going to shoot Caleb, so what was she doing?

"Listen to me." Caleb's voice took on a sense of urgency that frightened her. "Why don't we get out of this situation first, then we can put a call in to my boss and see what he can do to help? What do you—"

Gunfire erupted, cutting off whatever other argument he might have made, and he dove for her, dragging Ranger with him, and tucked her into a notch between the boulders. He shoved the big dog toward her and rolled. "Ranger, guard! Both of you stay down."

Ranger dropped to the ground between her and Caleb instantly, attention fully focused on Caleb.

On one knee, with his other foot planted firmly on the ground, Caleb took cover behind a boulder and aimed his own weapon at the gunmen, who'd at least stopped shooting—for the moment.

She clutched her weapon against her chest, unsure she'd even be able to fire if the men made it through Caleb and Ranger, both of whom had positioned themselves between her and danger. The fact that Caleb hadn't tried to take her gun before he turned his back on her offered at least a little comfort.

"Let's just see if these are the good guys," Caleb said, though it was clear he didn't think so. How could he when they'd already opened fire? Granted, she had been holding a weapon trained on them at the time. "Freeze! Police! Drop your weapons!"

Police? He'd told her he worked for a private investigation firm. Which was the truth? Either of them? Or was he lying to everyone?

If this man was a criminal, he was the most forgiving one she'd ever met. At least, that she could remember. The thought had a laugh bubbling out. She slapped a hand over her mouth. Had she gone crazy? That sure would explain a lot.

A barrage of gunfire interrupted any further contemplation of her sanity, or lack thereof.

She started to put her hands over her ears, block out the nightmare she'd awoken to, and realized the weapon was still in her hand. Bullets seemed to ricochet off everything around them, chipping boulders, tearing through brush, whizzing past far too close. This had to stop, or someone was going to get killed.

"Okay, so definitely not the good guys." Caleb shrugged

off his backpack as he returned fire and tossed it toward her. "Get me another clip out of the side pocket."

She opened one of a variety of pockets—nothing but beef jerky—patted some of the others until one seemed promising, then pulled out a clip. Her hand shook wildly as she held it out to him. "Here."

"Stay low while I reload." He ducked behind the boulder, ejected one clip and reloaded another at the speed of light, then returned to his position.

The gunmen must have paused to reload, too, as silence descended, leaving her ears ringing. Or maybe that was from the head wound. Either way, she wasn't about to cower there while whatever danger she'd brought with her threatened both Caleb and Ranger's lives simply because they were kind enough to stop and help a stranger. At least, she thought she was a stranger to them.

When the gunfire resumed, Olivia crept around the far side of the cropping, took a deep breath and aimed. She gripped the foreign-feeling weapon in both hands, her sweat-soaked palms making it difficult to keep a firm hold. Then she blew out a slow breath, fixed her gaze on the closer of the two gunmen trying to use a bush for cover and fired.

The unexpected recoil slammed through her arm and jerked the weapon up. Had she been caught off guard because she'd never fired a weapon, or because she forgot about the recoil along with everything else? It didn't matter. At least it seemed her survival instincts were still intact. She fired again, and again, even after the two gunmen ducked for cover and stopped firing.

"Hold up." Caleb laid a hand over hers. "Don't waste ammo."

She nodded—that made sense—then crouched with her back against the boulders and waited, sucking in painful breaths, working to steady her breathing.

"You okay?" Caleb kept his focus straight ahead, his aim steady, and squinted.

"Honestly? I have no idea." She'd clearly been involved in some kind of crash that had robbed her not only of her memories but of any sense of who she was. But had it even been an accident? Had the men who were shooting at her forced them off the road? She racked her brain, desperate for any kernel of information that she might grab hold of, but there was simply nothing.

"Stop trying so hard to remember." Caleb stood in front of her, tucked his gun back into the holster, then checked on Ranger.

Ranger stood at his side as if awaiting further instructions. Had she ever seen such a well-behaved dog?

Apparently satisfied Ranger hadn't been harmed, Caleb held out a hand to help her up. "It should be safe now. The two of them retreated."

She chanced a quick peek over the boulder. The men appeared to be gone. "What do you mean, stop trying to remember?"

He gestured toward her. "If the furrowed brows and clenched jaw are any indication, you're going to hurt yourself straining that hard."

"Do you have any idea what it's like to wake up completely unaware of who you are, where you are, where you came from, or even who might be an important part of your life? And then have to flee men armed with guns?" She dropped back onto her knees, wrapped her arms around herself, and rocked back and forth. She needed comfort, needed to move, needed to go back to her life before the accident. She needed a do-over.

She closed her eyes, and a vision of the accident scene came unbidden. "There was a man in the car when I climbed out. I don't even know who he was… He was probably the limo driver, but he could have been my husband, a coworker, my best friend, and I just left him lying there without a pulse, didn't even try to pull him out and do CPR."

She sobbed—did she know CPR?—then sucked in a deep breath.

Apparently accepting she wasn't ready to get up yet, Caleb lowered the hand he'd held out and crouched down in front of her, resting his arms comfortably on his knee. "Hey."

She didn't answer, too lost in what-ifs to deal with him.

He reached a hand toward her, then seemed to think better of the idea and let it drop. "Listen to me. Most likely, your amnesia isn't permanent. You've clearly been through something very traumatic, between the crash and the gunmen that seem to be after you, so I think maybe your mind is just taking a minute to process everything. I'm sure your memories will start to come back if you can try to calm down and relax."

"Calm down and relax? Did you seriously just say that to me?"

He shrugged. "Sorry, I'm not the best at conveying my thoughts, and I mean no offense, just that I think maybe you need to take a breath and try to let go of some of the tension if you want to remember."

A smile tugged at her. "And is that opinion based on any actual medical knowledge?"

"None whatsoever." He grinned. Obviously, Caleb Miller had mastered cool, calm and collected under pressure.

And somehow, she found herself smiling back at him. How strange, considering they'd been exchanging gunfire with criminals only seconds ago. Then again, *strange* seemed to define most of the day. Or maybe not. Maybe this was perfectly normal for her. "So, it's basically wishful thinking."

"How about we call it an educated guess?" He stood and held out his hand once more.

This time, she took it and let him help her up, then brushed the sand off her skirt and legs. "So, what now?"

"Let's start with the most important things and work our way down the list."

She nodded and wiped the tears from her cheeks, then realized she was still holding onto the gun. The thought of handing it over to Caleb flashed through her mind for an instant, then she tucked it back into her waistband. She had no idea if she was a distrusting person by nature, or if her total lack of memories had her too frightened to trust anyone, including herself.

"Other than the head injury, are you hurt?" He pointed to the blood on the front of her blouse.

She shook her head. "No. I don't think so. A little banged around, some bumps, bruises and cuts, but I think I'm okay."

"I have a first aid kit in my backpack. Will you let me at least try to stop the bleeding and bandage that head wound?" He made no move for the bag, simply waited for her answer.

She nodded again, then had to reach out a hand and

steady herself against the boulder when she felt a little lightheaded, whether from her injury, the stress or the heat, she had no idea. She did know she needed a moment to think.

Once again, he reached for her, before seemingly thinking better of the idea, then grabbed his backpack instead. He gestured behind her. "Why don't you sit on that flat rock over there, and we'll get you bandaged up so we can get out of here?"

Was it safe to stay put? Maybe they should move before the gunmen returned. But the thought of going anywhere with a stranger brought another rush of panic. She wondered if he'd guessed that, if that was why he suggested sitting there. Or perhaps he'd noticed how unsteady she was. Either way, she did as he instructed and sat, mostly because she was afraid she might fall over if she didn't. "And go where?"

"The hospital might be a good start."

"No!" She wasn't sure which of them was more surprised by the outburst, but everything in her screamed to stay away from the hospital. "I'm sorry. I'm not even sure why I'm so against the hospital, just that the thought terrifies me."

"Okay."

"That's it? Okay?" She wasn't sure what to make of the fact that he was so open to allowing her instincts to lead them. For some reason, the idea felt new to her.

He set the backpack next to her, rummaged through it and took out the first aid kit. "I figure you might not remember much, but whatever instincts are guiding you will probably lead you down the right path. Do you believe in God?"

"Yes, I do." The unexpected question threw her, but not nearly as much as the immediate and absolute certainty of her answer.

He gestured toward her neck, and she reached up, fingered the cross hanging there. Whoever she was, whatever was going on in her life, she had no doubt her faith in God remained strong. The reminder brought comfort. It was the first thing she'd found to hold onto.

"Good. So do I, even if I don't trust too many people. So, for now, the best we can do is go with your gut." He soaked a couple of gauze pads with antiseptic. "Which means, no hospital."

She started to nod, then caught herself as he tried to clean up the cut on her head. "Can I ask you something?"

"Uh-huh."

"Why are you helping me? How can you be sure I'm not a criminal?" What if she was? That thought brought even more fear than the fact that she was being hunted.

"I can't be sure. But if the gunmen after you were on the up and up, they never would have opened fire across the desert. Plus, they'd have holstered their weapons and come forward when I yelled police. The fact that they kept on shooting, then turned and fled, leads me to believe they are probably the bad guys in this situation."

"Huh. I hadn't thought of that." But now that he mentioned it, it made sense. She winced at the sting of the antiseptic he applied.

"The way I figure it, right now, you're just a person in need of help, and I happen to have the skills necessary to provide that help. Like I said, I believe in God. I believe He leads us exactly where we're supposed to be, precisely when we're meant to be there, *if* we are open and listening and willing to follow the path He lays out for us." Caleb taped a bandage to her head, then stepped back and propped his hands on his hips to study his work. "No matter what, you're still deserving of help. Besides, even if you are a criminal, we're both holding weapons. And of the two of us, I have a sneaking suspicion I'm more proficient."

She couldn't argue that, since she had a feeling he was right.

"Now..." He closed the first aid kit, shoved it into the backpack and looked around while he slung it onto his back. "Making them think I was a police officer may have bought us some time, but since we have no idea what we're up against, I suggest we get out of here fast before those two show up with reinforcements."

While Caleb was grateful Olivia, if that was the woman's name, had agreed to go with him, he was less than enthusiastic about trying to figure out what he was supposed to do with her. Checking on a fire he might have been able to put out or call in, even helping an accident victim until help could arrive, were things he could deal with. A woman with no memory of who she was or how she came to be the victim of what no longer appeared to be an accident was another story entirely. Especially this woman, wearing a skirt and high heels that screamed office worker rather than adventurer, who'd pulled herself out of a wrecked limousine. What was a woman like her doing out here in the first place? And who were the two gunmen chasing her? Stalkers? A hired hit—some rich businessman bored with his socialite wife? She wasn't wearing a wedding ring, but still...

He caught himself, then let go of the interest she'd

piqued. He and Ranger were supposed to be taking a break, recuperating, not getting embroiled in another case.

And yet, he fully believed what he told her. What were the chances of him and Ranger stumbling across a woman wandering the California desert, covered in blood, with no memory of who she was or where she came from? He honestly believed he was in this desert at the exact time she found herself in danger because he was meant to help her. Which meant he was going to have to see this through, at least until he could find someone who could take care of her. He sighed and tipped his hat farther back on his head.

"Is everything okay?" she asked.

"What? Oh, sorry. Yes, everything's fine. Just trying to figure out what to do and where to go from here." They'd walked most of the mile back to his RV in silence—no easy task for her, wearing high-heeled shoes since the sand was too hot and rocky to walk barefoot. But she hadn't complained once. Nor had she said anything else.

Not that he could blame her; she had to be confused and terrified, especially when she seemed more Rodeo Drive than Mojave Desert. As it was, it had taken him showing her his driver's license, several credit cards and his Jameson Investigations business card before she'd agreed to walk with him back to his RV. And that was after she'd flat out refused to return to the accident scene where police, firefighters and paramedics would have been available to take her off his hands.

Ranger walked between them, and Olivia occasionally reached down and smoothed her fingers over his ears or weaved them into the fur on his head. She didn't seem to fear him at all. Nor should she. Ranger was a great dog, a hero, really. But he was big and unfamiliar to her. Yet, the two walked together side by side as if they'd known each other forever, as if she instinctively trusted Ranger in a way she couldn't trust Caleb. It almost made him wish they'd met under different, less dire circumstances.

But now, with darkness descending on the desert, no idea where the two gunmen had disappeared to and a woman who clearly needed medical attention, the stakes had increased exponentially. "If it's okay with you, I have to call my boss and check in. He was supposed to send first responders to the scene of the accident, and he might have some information to share with us by now."

She chewed on her lower lip so hard he was afraid she might gnaw a hole right through it.

"Listen, Olivia, you are going to need more help than just me. Even if the two of us work together—" which he hadn't yet decided to do "—there's more involved here than we can handle alone."

She nodded. "I suppose."

"Let me call Zac Jameson and see if he can help. He has resources I can't access on my own." Caleb would make the call even without her approval, but it might go toward earning her trust if he could convince her to agree first.

She sniffed and nodded, seemingly trying to convince herself. "Okay."

"Great." He pulled out his phone and entered the PIN to unlock it before she could change her mind. Because if she did, Caleb would be stuck there with her. No way was he leaving anyone out in the desert alone and in danger.

She lowered her gaze to the ground. "I just want you to know, I'm sorry."

His finger hovered over the number as he shifted to look at her. "Sorry for what?"

"For messing up your…" Her eyes narrowed in suspicion, as if suddenly realizing something. "What were you doing out here, anyway?"

"Ranger and I were having some much-needed downtime." No way was he going into the catastrophe that had led to his need for space. He wasn't ready to share the intimate details of the search that had only turned up body after body. He wasn't ready to talk about the fact that they hadn't found a single survivor amid the rubble that remained of the building that came crashing down atop dozens of people. Would it have made a difference if he'd been there? Would Ranger have detected the bomb before it went off?

There was no going back, no changing how things had gone down. Why was it he could so easily accept that God had led him to the desert to save Olivia, but he couldn't accept the losses as anything other than his own fault?

Anyway…that was a philosophy to contemplate another time. Maybe when he returned to his solitude once he delivered Olivia safely to Zac Jameson.

"What's going on? I tried to reach you," Zac answered.

"Sorry, Zac. We ran into a bit of a situation out here."

"We?"

"Ranger and I found a woman walking in the desert, covered in blood. She says there was a man in the car with her who didn't make it and that she escaped, but she's extremely frightened. Before we could talk much, two gunmen showed up and opened fire." Caleb scanned the horizon even as he spoke, searching every nook, cranny and shadow they could have secreted themselves in.

"Where are they now?"

"I don't know. When I called out that I was a police officer, we exchanged fire, and then they took off."

"All right. Okay. Did you return with the woman to the authorities at the scene?"

Caleb winced, knowing that was exactly what he should have done. "Not exactly. She's terrified. She doesn't want to go to the hospital or back to the scene. With the two men gunning for her, I figured it might be best to trust her instincts and keep a low profile for a minute while we figure things out."

"Who is she?" Zac asked.

"That's the thing—she doesn't know. She suffered a head injury and says she has amnesia." Not that he'd noticed any indication she might be faking it, but you never knew. Maybe she was an actress, putting on a performance so he'd help her out of a difficult situation.

At that point, it would have made perfect sense for Zac to question Caleb's choice to flee again, but he wouldn't. Zac trusted every last one of his agents completely. Now if only Caleb could find that same level of trust in himself. The open line was quiet but for a steady *rat-a-tat-tat* Caleb was sure came from Zac tapping a pen against the nearest object, as he was prone to do while thinking.

"I have to admit," Zac finally said, "I'm intrigued."

Yes! Caleb resisted the urge to pump his fist. When something intrigued Zac Jameson, he was worse than Ranger with a bone.

"So, how do you want to handle it?" Zac asked.

Caleb wanted to return to his RV, have some dinner and relax under the starlight, but that wasn't going to happen. Not yet, anyway. "I was hoping you'd have an idea. And, since leaving the scene of the accident is technically a crime, I was also hoping you'd reach out to the local authorities."

"I could do that. Considering there were extenuating circumstances, they might be okay as long as she's reaching out through us." *Tap, tap, tap. Tap, tap, tap.* "I'll tell you what, why don't you bring her in? I'll set up a safe house and have a medical team ready when you arrive. Then we'll see if we can get a positive ID on her or the other victim and take it from there."

Caleb didn't want to admit, even to himself—especially to himself—how relieved he was that the responsibility for her wouldn't rest squarely on his shoulders. "That would be good."

"All right. When will you be here?"

He glanced at his watch and calculated. They were only a few minutes from the RV, then he'd have to drive to the airfield where he'd left Jameson Investigations' state-of-the-art Cessna turboprop, which he'd flown to California. It would take them roughly eight hours to fly to Florida, plus a refueling stop in Texas. At least he would get to enjoy the tranquility that soaring through the clouds brought. "By tomorrow, probably around lunchtime."

"All right. I'll be in touch." With that, Zac disconnected the call.

Caleb stuffed the phone back into his pocket. "He wants me to bring you to a safe house he'll set up where you can be treated by a doctor. Once we get there, we can take your fingerprints and try to figure who you are."

She eyed him, her scrutiny skeptical. "Where is the safe house?"

"In Florida, where Jameson Investigations is based."

"And where are we now?"

His heart tripped. How could he have forgotten she wouldn't even know where she was? And what would it feel like for your head to be so…empty? "We're in California, but it's probably best to put some distance between you and them, buy us some time and space until we can figure all of this out. But if you're not comfortable with that, Zac can set something up out here for you."

She stopped walking and stood perfectly still, then turned to him and smiled, a radiant smile that hinted at the woman she might be when not burdened by all of this. Maybe she *was* a movie star. That would explain what she was doing in a limo and running around the desert in a skirt and heels. "Yes, that would be good."

He studied her for a moment. How did she go from threatening to shoot him, to flying across the country with him in the span of an hour? "Do you know someone in Florida?"

She shrugged, and when her smile widened, her blue eyes sparkled with a hint of mischief. "I have no idea, but you said to go with what feels right, and I can't explain why, but that does."

"Okay, then." He'd get her to the safe house, let Zac's team take over, and Caleb would move on with his life, provided no one else got in their way, of course. "Works for me."

THREE

Olivia stopped short at the sight of the aircraft, if you could call it that, Caleb led her toward at the small airfield. She balked, insisting it looked more like a toy plane than an actual aircraft. She seriously wanted to consider alternative forms of transportation. But what? She couldn't fly commercial without any ID. And if she owned any, which she assumed she must, it had been lost in the crash. No one would rent her a car without a driver's license. She even considered a train, but they didn't have time, because she might not know much, but a sense of urgency battered her relentlessly.

She had no idea if she was afraid of flying in general or just of the tiny plane, especially in the dead of night. But either way, the terror that gripped her abated as the country unfolded beneath them.

They flew for about four hours before stopping at an airfield somewhere in the Midwest, refueling and taking a much needed break to stretch their legs and let Ranger do his business in the warm dawn light. A few hours later, they were still aloft. The sky was an incredibly brilliant blue, and puffy white clouds stacked atop one another like giant piles of cotton.

For a moment, she wished the circumstances were different, and Caleb wasn't her bodyguard but a man she might enjoy getting to know. He seemed like a nice enough guy, giving up his vacation to take her to a safe house.

Of course, for all she knew, Zac Jameson would charge her a fortune for the protection. Did she have it? Just because she was riding in a limo didn't necessarily mean she had money.

"Did you manage to get some sleep?"

She jumped, startled by Caleb's voice.

"Sorry. I didn't mean to scare you."

"No, it's all right." She waved off the apology. She was in a fair amount of pain. Her head throbbed relentlessly. Every muscle in her body screamed in protest whenever she tried to move, and even when she didn't. It seemed that her tumble down the mountainside followed up by running for her life and trekking across the desert had taken its toll. But she didn't need to unload all of that on him. "I'm just a little on edge."

"That's certainly understandable." He checked some gauges, fiddled with something else, then resumed looking out the windshield. Apparently, he wasn't much of a talker.

Was she? Who knew? She'd spent most of the flight so far quietly sitting with her head back and her eyes closed, racking her brain for some sort of knowledge, praying some of the pain would soon ease so she could think more clearly. Even if she couldn't remember her name, she must have some knowledge, some talent. Was she an artist? An accountant? A stunt double? There had to be some kind of information rattling around in her empty head. But if there was, it remained stubbornly elusive.

Ranger left his dog bed in the back and poked his head between the seats.

When she laid a hand against his face, he tilted into her touch. Did she have a dog? If she didn't, it was going on her to-do list…as soon as she figured out where she lived. "How long have you had Ranger?"

"Four years. I got him when he was a puppy and trained him to work with me."

"He's amazing."

Caleb ruffled the fur on Ranger's head, the look he gave him filled with affection. "Yeah, he is."

And with that, they promptly ran out of conversation, and silence descended, the weight of it uncomfortable. Olivia shifted in her seat and cringed at the various aches and tugs, getting antsy after sitting still for so long. Something caught against the seat belt. She patted her skirt pocket and realized something was in it. ID? How could she have missed that?

Excited for the first time that she might learn her identity, she reached into her pocket and pulled out two items— a flash drive and a photo. Odd. She patted her other pocket but found nothing, so she turned her attention to the photo. In it, a woman sat at a table, a laptop beside her open to a news channel. The day's date was prominent on the screen. "Do you know what today's date is?"

"The fourth, why?" Caleb glanced in her direction, then frowned. "Who's that?"

The picture was dated the third. Yesterday, the same day she crashed. Why would she be carrying a picture around in her pocket? Along with a flash drive? She tucked the drive back into her pocket; she couldn't do anything with it unless she found a computer. The fact that she realized that sparked a small flare of hope, but she'd examine that later.

Instead, she turned her attention to the photo—the woman in particular. Her long blond hair hung limp, and her eyes were puffy and red, as if she'd been crying. Did Olivia know her? Frustration beat at her. She had to know the woman. Why else would she have the photo? She studied the background, every inch of it, but there were no signs to indicate where it had been taken.

"Do you know her?" Caleb craned his neck to see the photo.

For some reason, his curiosity irked her. She folded the picture in half and stuffed it back into her pocket. "I have no idea."

She scrubbed her hands over her face and into the tangled blond mess of her hair…

Wait! She pulled the photo out again. Could it be her in the picture? The woman's hair was straight. Olivia's was wavy, even after crashing and traipsing through the desert with nothing more than her fingers to comb through the tangles. Still… She had found a gun next to the limo, had even wondered if she'd been kidnapped. Was the picture a ransom demand? Was there someone, somewhere, frantic to learn of her whereabouts while trying to get together a ransom to save her?

She held the photo out to Caleb. "I know this sounds stupid, but could it be me?"

He narrowed his eyes and studied it. "No. It's not you, but I have to admit, there is a resemblance. A relative, maybe? Sister? Cousin?"

She shook her head, more out of frustration than in answer, then tucked the photo away more carefully. As horrible as it would have been to find out she'd been kidnapped, at least it would have answered some of her questions. Plus, something that traumatic in addition to the car accident certainly would explain her amnesia. "I just don't know."

"Hey." Caleb squeezed her wrist before returning his hand to the controls. "Don't worry about anything yet. Once we get you to the doctor, we'll see what he says and take it from there."

"Easy for you to say." She appreciated the sentiment but made light of it, not wanting to get into any deep conversations about her feelings, especially not with a stranger. She didn't even know what her feelings were, other than scared.

She turned and looked out the window as they soared over forests full of towering trees, some of which seemed prehistoric, as if untouched by man, pure and filled with wildlife, just as God had made them. "How much longer?"

"About half an hour. Not long now. Does anything look familiar?"

She stared out the window. It certainly was beautiful, but she couldn't say it was familiar in anyway. "No, I don't think—"

Several loud popping sounds interrupted, and she glanced over to see what Caleb was doing.

He looked over his shoulder out the side window.

"What's wrong?"

"I'm not sure." His gaze returned to the gauges she had no clue how to interpret, and he frowned, his eyes narrowed in concentration.

Then a loud boom had her grabbing hold of her seat. "What was that?"

"Hold tight."

Flames erupted from the front of the plane. Smoke

poured from somewhere, inhibiting the view out the windshield.

"Caleb?" Olivia braced her feet against the floor. "Please, tell me what's happening."

He shifted his headset microphone in front of his mouth. "Mayday. Mayday."

Her mind shut down. She might not know much, but she definitely knew mayday wasn't a good thing. She waited for him to relay their position before asking again. "Please, Caleb. What is going on?"

"I'm pretty sure someone is trying to shoot us down."

"Shoot…" The breath rushed from her lungs, and all she could manage was a wheezed, "But how?"

"I don't know yet. But we have to deal with the crisis first. We can figure out what happened afterward."

If we survive. Like him, she kept that part to herself. "What are we going to do?"

"I can put the Cessna down if I can find an open field long enough to land in, but in this section of forest, that's not likely."

"So what else can we do?"

"Okay, I know you can't remember anything, but I need you to close your eyes and envision something and tell me if you think you've ever done it before or if it sounds like something you might enjoy. Okay?"

Like they had time for that right now. She inhaled deeply, blew the air out on a slow count of four. He probably wouldn't be asking her to do this right now if it weren't urgent. And they were running out of time. She squeezed her eyes closed, then worked to relax them. Laying her head back, as she had for most of the trip, she took one more deep breath. "Okay. Go ahead."

"So, do you think maybe you've ever gone skydiving?"

Her eyes shot open, and she lurched upright. Her voice came out in a high-pitched squeak. "What? You've got to be kidding me."

He quirked a brow at her. "I'm guessing that's a no?"

How could he be so calm? Could he really be sitting there that casually talking about jumping out of an airplane? "No. I mean, yes. I mean, yes, that's a no. Besides, what about Ranger? You can't leave him in the plane when it goes down!"

Because if he could do that, she'd completely misjudged him and made a terrible mistake going with him.

"Ranger is trained to skydive with me, but I don't have time to give you a lesson, and I can't tandem dive with both of you."

The ground rushed up at them. "Please, tell me there's a plan B."

"There sure is." He grinned, setting alight a pair of eyes the same bluish green as the lake they were currently free-falling toward. "Hold on tight and pray."

Caleb wrestled the controls, desperately trying to reach the barren field in the distance, knowing there was no way he'd make it. He'd already notified the proper authorities, as well as Zac Jameson. With no chance to parachute out, he had no choice but to try to land as gently as possible. "Ranger, bed."

He obeyed instantly, trotting to the crate Zac kept secured to the fuselage in the back of the plane.

"Down."

He lowered himself to the dog bed, which would cushion him at least somewhat from the impact.

Olivia's eyes were wide open as she braced herself, then glanced over her shoulder at Ranger. "He'll be okay?"

"Yes." He prayed he was right, and they'd all walk away from this. He wouldn't make the field, and the instant he hit the towering pine trees, the bed of needles covering the ground beneath them was likely to go up in flames. They might set the whole forest on fire. It was the dry season in Florida, and he'd already seen a couple of smoke plumes from forest fires in the distance on their way in. Even with emergency vehicles surely on their way, they would have to move fast. "Is your seat belt on tight?"

She checked it and responded with a calm, "Yes."

He spared her a quick glance. She seemed to be holding herself together. "As soon as the plane stops, I need you to unbuckle and follow my instructions to the letter."

She nodded. "Got it."

"Okay." He checked Ranger, held the plane as steady as he could and aimed for a gap between the trees. All the swamps and lakes in Florida, and they had to go down on fire in the middle of a pine forest. "Please, God, help me get us down in one piece."

"Amen."

Her acknowledgment surprised him, though he couldn't say why, since she'd already told him she believed in God. Maybe he just hadn't expected an answer. But it was a comfort to know he wasn't the only one praying. "Here goes nothing."

They hit the trees hard, tearing through the upper branches. Olivia clapped her hands over her ears.

He fought to keep the nose up. One wing hit a massive oak and sent them skittering sideways. The tail hit another tree and bounced them back. The sounds of banging and tearing drowned out everything else, but he never heard Olivia scream or cry out. Had she passed out? Hit her head again? He couldn't check her yet as he maneuvered the plane to the ground.

And then they were down, the plane bouncing along the carpet of pine needles to a stop. He yanked off his seat belt. "Hey! You okay?"

She clutched the seat in a white-knuckled grip and nodded. The cut on her head had opened up again, and blood poured down the side of her face from beneath the bandage.

"We have to get out."

She nodded again but stayed where she was.

"Olivia. Hey." He bent over her and undid the seat belt himself. Then gently but firmly gripped her upper arm. "Hon, I wouldn't move you if I didn't have to, but those pines are going to ignite and burn rapidly. We can't stay here."

"Right. Yeah. Okay." She stood on her own, followed him to the door.

He quickly helped Ranger into his booties and vest, which he'd taken off during the flight. Slinging his backpack over his shoulder, he grabbed a first aid kit from the plane to replenish what he'd used from the one in his backpack. He didn't have time to salvage anything else. "Come on."

Between the two of them, they managed to get the door unstuck and open. Caleb climbed out first, scanning the area before reaching up to help Olivia.

She stood in the doorway, shivering in the mid-afternoon Florida heat. "What if they're still out there?"

"They shot at us miles ago. It would take them a while to reach us, even with all-terrain vehicles." Unless, of course, there were others who'd gone ahead, but there was no way anyone could have anticipated exactly how far he'd manage to get after being hit. He could have nose-dived straight down. Instead, he'd been able to keep the plane in the air long enough to make a sort of safe landing.

Without another word, she leaned over and gripped his shoulders, then let him lift her down. She leaned back against the mangled fuselage.

"Stay right there." He called for Ranger.

Ranger jumped out and stood beside him, waiting for a command.

Caleb hooked an arm around Olivia's waist, wrapping her arm over his shoulder, and started away from the plane. Once he'd moved her and Ranger a safe distance, he told them to wait and started back toward the burning fuselage.

"Wait. Where are you going?" A tremor shook her voice, and he regretted having to leave her alone and afraid in the middle of the forest. At least in the desert, you could see someone coming. Here, every bush and tree could conceal an attacker.

"I have fire extinguishers in the plane. I want to see if I can douse the flames before this whole forest goes up. I'll be right back." He jogged back and hoisted himself up through the doorway, then grabbed two of the fire extinguishers. Only one was required, but Zac kept at least three in each of his planes. A good idea, considering the sort of high-risk operations they often conducted. When he turned, Olivia leaned in the doorway.

She held out her hands. "Give me one."

With no time to argue, he did as she asked. Then he grabbed the other two. Working together they managed to suppress the flames.

When she'd emptied her extinguisher, Olivia leaned back against a tree and swiped the hair out of her face. "Now what do we do? Wait here for help?"

"Normally, I'd say yes, but the smoke billowing out of this thing is like a beacon announcing our position to anyone who might want to find us."

She straightened quickly and looked around. "How can you be sure someone did this? Maybe there was just something wrong with the plane."

"I might have agreed, if not for the damage to the side of the fuselage." He pointed toward a hole running along the tail section.

"You're sure it's not from crashing into the trees?"

He laughed. "Not unless the oaks and pines were carrying a Stinger."

She lowered her gaze, letting the hair fall back over her face. "I'm so sorry, Caleb."

"Sorry? For what?"

"For bringing all of this on you and for putting you and Ranger in harm's way." She laid a hand on Ranger's head, though whether to comfort him or herself, Caleb had no idea. Probably a little of both.

"Hey." He tipped her chin up so she had no choice but to look at him, then tucked a strand of hair from in front of her face behind her ear. "This is not your fault, Olivia. The blame for all of this lies squarely on the shoulders of whoever is after you."

"You can't know that," she sobbed, then added quietly, "I don't even know that. What if I did something to bring this on myself?"

"Look. I don't know you, and I have no idea what you might or might not have done. But here's what I've learned about you in less than twenty-four hours. Back in the desert, you could have stayed hidden behind the boulders where I'd secreted you and depended on me to keep you safe. Instead, you studied the situation, then took cover and opened fire with a weapon you are clearly uncomfortable using. When our plane was going down, and you had to be understandably terrified for your life, your first concern was for Ranger, a dog you'd only just met." Which earned her a lot of points in his book. "Then, when I returned to get the fire extinguishers, you were right there lending a hand, even though I told you to wait a distance away where you would be safe."

She shrugged.

He tugged her hair, trying to lighten the mood. "Bad people don't do things like that, Olivia. I have no idea how you wound up in this position, but we're going to figure it out. Now, come on. Let's move before they find us again."

They started through the forest, branches and burrs clawing them as they walked. "You do think it's the same people who were after me in the desert, right?"

He shrugged, his mind racing. He had to contact Zac and have Angela ping his satellite phone so they could arrange an extraction. "I had to file a flight plan. They could have gotten access to that. Heck, anyone with internet access and a cell phone can track a flight nowadays."

"I guess." She continued to walk, not quite steady on her feet, and he hooked an arm around her waist.

"Lean on me if you need to. Are you hurt anywhere else but your head?"

"My legs and feet hurt, but I'll be okay. No doubt from trudging through the desert and now the forest in Ralph Lauren pumps."

Was her memory returning? That had to be a good sign. Although, what kind of prima donna would you have to be for your shoe brand to be the first memory to return? "You remember the brand name of your shoes?"

She laughed, and he enjoyed the sound, musical in the expanse of forest, as if she belonged there. "No, silly. I took them off before to dump the sand out, and the name was written on the inside."

He laughed. Not a prima donna at all. At least she had a sense of humor and maintained it despite less than ideal circumstances. He caught himself, realizing some level of trust for this woman had begun to emerge—a stranger he'd found wandering the desert with a couple of gunmen after her. She carried a picture of a woman that for all intents and purposes appeared to be a ransom photo. He'd never have left her behind to fend for herself, but he'd do well to remember trusting her was off the table.

It wasn't like he had amnesia. He remembered full well what trusting someone had gotten him in the past. It was time to reinforce his barriers, maintain his distance and keep in mind this was a strictly professional relationship. "Here, why don't we rest for a couple of minutes? There's a downed log over there you can sit on."

He guided her to the log beside a lake and checked for snakes, alligators and other critters that might have made their homes underneath. He handed her a water bottle from his backpack, then filled Ranger's bowl and finally took a swig of his own water. Warm but at least it would keep them hydrated.

Ranger finished drinking, then looked up into the trees and barked.

Caleb shot to his feet as a troop of gray and brown

monkeys screeched and dove from the surrounding trees. They swung from branch to branch, rolling and playing after being disturbed.

Olivia laughed and jumped up, clapping her hands together. She watched them frolic in the cypress trees along the lake's shore. "Aren't they great?"

He made his home in New York, wherever his work with Jameson Investigations took him, so he didn't know much about Florida wildlife other than to watch out for gators and venomous snakes. Oh, and bears. "I didn't realize there were monkeys in Central Florida."

"Sure." She nodded, full of enthusiasm. "They're rhesus macaques, not native to Florida, but brought in and released in the 1930s on an island in Silver River, to—" She froze, her eyes going wide.

Caleb gripped her arms. "Do you know how you know that?"

"No." She squinted up at the monkeys, shook her head. "I have no idea. It just came to me."

"Well, if one thing came back to you, I'm sure more will follow. Now, let's get out of here." *Before our attackers catch up to us again.*

FOUR

Olivia tried to watch every direction at once—not that the acres and acres of prehistoric forest looked any different no matter where she looked. Knowing an attack could come from anywhere at any time had her more on edge than she cared to admit. Especially in light of the clear, calm manner in which Caleb seemed to accept and deal with everything that came their way.

Though she had no doubt her faith was strong, she couldn't help but wonder if it was strong enough to lead her through whatever might come next. The fact that she'd made it as far as she had awed her. Even without knowing anything about herself, she didn't view herself as strong. Not weak, either, but not particularly valiant or courageous. And definitely frightened.

Caleb, on the other hand, barely blinked in the face of danger. The calm he exuded while crash landing that plane made him a hero in her mind. Instead of panicking, he simply uttered a prayer and did what had to be done.

She could take a lesson from him. If she could ever remember what exactly had to be done. Something… A sense of purpose drove her, strengthening her resolve. A mission of some sort? Wisps of fragmented memories, blurry images that skittered away every time she tried to grasp hold, teased her.

Her ankle twisted, ripping her from her reverie. She staggered and caught herself against a tree trunk, barely managing to remain upright.

Ranger barked once and stopped beside her.

Caleb glanced over, then told whomever he was speaking to on the phone to hold on. "You okay?"

"Yeah. Sorry." She straightened, then turned to lean her back against the tree, taking the weight off her bad ankle. "I just need a minute."

"Sure." He scanned the forest as he returned to his call.

That was it? Sure? What about the potential danger lurking around every tree and shrub? What about the fact that they were lost in a forest with a pack of gunmen on their heels? What about the fact that she had no idea who she was or what she was supposed to be doing?

Her gaze shot from tree to tree, from shadow to shadow. Looking for danger, yes, but maybe more importantly wondering why a forest thousands of miles from where she assumed she lived seemed so familiar and comforting? She stifled a sob of frustration.

Caleb disconnected his call and stuffed the phone back into his pocket. "Can you walk?"

Could she? She had no idea. But she did know she wasn't about to stand there feeling sorry for herself until someone showed up and killed them. She straightened and eased her weight tentatively onto the ankle she'd twisted. No stabbing pain, but a dull ache throbbed in time with her quickened heart rate. She let go of the tree and shifted her weight onto her other foot, then took a step. "I think I can. I just twisted my ankle. It's these stupid shoes."

"If you're having a hard time, I can fashion a stretcher from branches and palm fronds, and Ranger and I can pull you." He reached for her arm when she took another hesitant step. "Or, I can wrap the ankle with a bandage from the first aid kit."

The fact that he was offering but hadn't made a move to unshoulder the backpack containing the kit told her all she needed to know. If he thought it was safe to hunker down where they were, he'd have already found somewhere for her to sit as he had in the desert even though there had still clearly been some risk.

"I'm fine." She started to walk, slower than before, more cautious where she stepped, but at least they were once again moving forward. Toward what danger, she had no idea. "Thank you, though."

"Sure. Ranger, heel." He walked next to her, arms at his sides, Ranger close by him, ready to catch her if she went down.

And suddenly, she couldn't stand it, hated being viewed as a victim. "So, who was on the phone?"

He studied her for a moment, then returned to surveilling their surroundings as he let her set the pace. "Angela Ryan."

"Who's that?"

"She's one of Zac's agents, works side by side with him. I had her locate my phone so they can send a rescue team." He glanced at her, shifted his gaze to her feet, then met her stare. "The nearest place they can land is about three miles from here. Do you honestly think you can walk that far?"

She blew out a breath and shifted her gaze away. Not that she noted any judgment in his eyes, but he seemed perceptive enough to pick up on the fear and doubt as well as the pain racking her. "I can walk however far we have to walk. But I cannot walk another step in these shoes."

Her next two steps were out of the arch-and-ankle-killing pumps. She left them where they were, then paused, glanced behind her and went back for them. Not that she cared about the shoes, but she wouldn't just leave them there in the forest. The first donation bin they came across, though, and she was tossing them in.

The carpet of pine needles, dry as they were, still felt good beneath her feet. She might have to tread more carefully so as not to step on anything, but her feet practically wept with relief. And her pace increased. Her ankle still ached, and her feet had blisters on top of the blisters, but that she could deal with.

Caleb laughed and shook his head. "It's about time."

"Yeah, well, the risk of walking any farther in these shoes finally outweighed the risk of stepping on a rattler."

He scanned the ground, the humor fading from his eyes as wariness crept in.

It was her turn to laugh. "Not big on the Florida wildlife, are you?"

He shrugged. "I like wildlife just fine. But I'm from New York, where the wildlife consists of pigeons, alley cats, and an occasional rat in the subway. Sometimes, when I'm walking along somewhere peaceful, the thought of dangerous wildlife slips my mind. Plus, Ranger usually warns me if there's something I need to worry about. How about you?"

She pondered the question for a moment, but when no answers were forthcoming, she changed the subject. "How long until the chopper lands?"

He glanced at his watch. "It won't be long now. By the

time we make it to the clearing, they should already be there."

She nodded, relieved the cavalry was on its way and they would no longer be on their own. "So, what do you usually do with your downtime?"

His grin brought an answering smile from her. "Actually, this is pretty much what I do all the time. When Ranger and I do take a break, we like to enjoy the outdoors, somewhere calm, peaceful and isolated."

"Well, it doesn't get much more isolated than this."

He paused and held out a hand for her to stop, then pointed ahead of them.

She responded instantly, coming to an immediate halt, and lifted her gaze from the ground where she'd be diligently searching for obstacles, to the direction he'd indicated. A wisp of smoke drifted into the sky. Had they gotten turned around? "Is that from our plane?"

He shook his head and laid a finger against his full lips.

She crouched low, listening intently for the telltale crunch of footsteps amid the dry brush. The reminder of the current conditions had a chill racing up her spine.

Finally, seeming satisfied no one posed an immediate threat, Caleb pointed to two more increasingly thick smoke columns. "Our plane is behind us. Even if the fire did reignite, it's not in this direction. And the fact that the smoke seems to be popping up in a line to the east makes me think it's no accident."

"Someone is setting fires?"

He nodded and looked back in the direction they'd come. "Yes, either to flush us out or to trap us."

"What are we going to do? Can we still make it to the chopper?"

He used a hand to shield his eyes from the sun. "Would you be okay here for a few minutes by yourself?"

He wanted to leave her behind? What if he didn't come back? What if the line of fire separated them and she was left alone surrounded by flames? She laid a trembling hand on Ranger's head.

"I just want to scout ahead a little."

She nodded. No way would she admit to being terrified of him leaving her. She barely knew him. "That's fine."

"I need to take Ranger with me."

She reluctantly lifted her hand from his warm fur. "Of course."

"Stay low and out of sight until we get back, okay?" The sincerity and concern in his gaze had tears pricking the backs of her eyes.

She nodded, unable to meet his gaze lest he recognize her sheer terror or the tears threatening to fall.

"Hey." He tipped her chin toward him. "I promise I will be right back."

"I'm good." She stepped back from his touch. She didn't know this man. He'd stood between her and danger more than once, had no doubt saved her life, and yet, he was still a stranger. The reminder left her chilled despite the scorching Florida heat.

She listened to his retreating footsteps against the dry brush that would no doubt fuel the flames he was running toward. Seemed that was Caleb's way—running toward danger when others would flee. When she could no longer hear his footfalls, she listened for their return. She stuck her hands into her skirt pockets, her fingers jamming against the flash drive. Something important? It had to be, didn't it?

She leaned her back against a tree, scanned the area, then focused inward, trying to imagine herself putting the drive into her pocket. A vague image emerged—her slipping the drive out of a computer, sticking it in her skirt pocket—but that was all. No sense of her mood or frame of mind. It could just as easily contain a movie she'd been watching as some deep, dark, world-changing secret. Frustrated, she rubbed a hand over her face and began to pace.

While focusing inward, she'd missed more columns of smoke popping up. Earlier, Caleb and Ranger had taken off at a full-out run. No doubt they could escape the flames without her hindering their speed. But would he leave her there? Probably not, if his actions so far were any indication. Caleb Miller was either an adrenaline junkie or the most selfless, courageous man she'd ever—

She cut the thought short. She had no idea what kind of men she'd met. Though, the fact that she'd ended up at the bottom of a cliff in a wrecked limo and been shot at multiple times didn't bode well. Unless, of course, there was a man out there somewhere, a good man, like Caleb, who was awaiting instructions to pay a ransom and have her returned to him. But that just didn't feel right.

The sound of Caleb's retuning footsteps saved her from having to contemplate a past that was nothing more than an empty book, filled with blank page after blank page. Would she ever recover her memories? Or was she doomed to the life she began yesterday when she awoke to the smell of smoke. An odor which she suddenly realized had increased exponentially in the time Caleb had been gone.

Another thought intruded. She had assumed she was hearing Caleb returning. What if it wasn't him? What if her attackers had found her once again, alone, unarmed, vulnerable? She took a step back, grabbed a dead branch that would probably disintegrate if she had to hit anyone with it and faced whoever or whatever was coming.

The sound of something crashing through the brush behind her had her whirling around. Threats from both sides? That couldn't be good.

She turned until a large oak was at her back, offering at least some protection, then braced herself, hefted the stick higher and prayed her ankle wouldn't give out. And that gunmen with automatic weapons wouldn't converge on her. If that happened, her weak ankle would be the least of her problems.

Frantic barking reached her. Ranger? Or had her pursuers brought dogs to track them in the forest?

Ranger leaped over a fallen tree trunk, dirt and dead leaves flying as he barreled toward her, his deep growls punctuating the barks. When he reached her, he stood in front of her, legs splayed, and continued to bark in the direction of the crashing brush behind her.

She whirled and stood at his side, ready for whatever threat would emerge. "It's okay, Ranger. What's wrong, boy? Where's Caleb?"

She chanced a glance over her shoulder just as he came into view.

The sounds behind her grew louder. Something grunted. Ranger lunged.

She dropped her branch and grabbed his vest, yanking him up short as a giant boar charged through the bushes, narrowly missing Ranger's flank.

The powerful animal skidded, his back legs almost going out from under him, then regained his footing.

Ranger spun around, and Olivia lost her grip on him.

"Ranger, stop!" Caleb yelled.

The boar hit Caleb's hip, knocking him off his feet. Even as he went airborne, Caleb reached for Ranger.

The boar kept going.

Ranger retreated to Caleb's side, continuing his incessant barking. Whether to alert his owner to danger or scare away any threats, Olivia had no idea.

She ran to Caleb, then dropped to her knees when she reached him curled on his side on the forest floor. "How bad are you hurt?"

Caleb moaned as he rolled onto his back, then eased himself up on an elbow, moving slowly and then pausing to assess the pain. When he pressed a hand against the wound, it came away covered in blood.

They had to get the bleeding stopped. Zac's team would be there soon, and they'd get Caleb the medical attention he needed, as long as she could keep him from bleeding out while they hiked close to three miles to reach the chopper. There was no way she could carry him, though the stretcher he'd suggested earlier might do the trick if they had more time.

He struggled to get the backpack off, and Olivia helped him untangle it from his arms and set it aside. Then she half dragged him while he used his heels to push himself backward until he slumped against a tree. She ripped open the backpack and fumbled out the first aid kit. "How bad is it?"

"I'll be all right." He shifted and hissed through his teeth.

"I'm sorry. I shouldn't have stopped Ranger from attacking. I was afraid he'd get hurt, so I grabbed his vest, and I didn't realize you were so close behind him, and…" Stupid. She'd acted instinctively without thinking about the consequences. Was that something she was often guilty of? Maybe that explained her current predicament. And now, Caleb was paying an even worse price for getting mixed up with her. She should just get him and Ranger to the helicopter and then head out on her own, fix whatever mess she'd made without involving anyone else.

She wiped tears from her cheeks with her wrist, soaked two large gauze pads with saline and handed them to him. "I shouldn't have interfered when he would have protected you. I'm so sorry. I'm sorry for everything."

Caleb pressed the bandages against the long, jagged tear that ran from his hip up his side to the bottom of his ribcage. Almost instantly, the blood soaked through them. "Hey."

She sniffed, ripping open more bandages at a frantic pace.

"Olivia." He gently stilled her hand. "Hey."

She finally paused and looked at him. Her hands trembled beneath his.

"Three things—one, I'm going to be fine. Two, you did exactly the right thing. If Ranger had attacked the boar, he'd have gotten hurt, or worse. Dogs who hunt boar require special training, and Ranger doesn't have it. He'd have defended me, but it would not have ended well for him."

She sucked in a shaky breath and nodded. "I don't understand. Why did it attack?"

"I don't think he did."

Seriously?

"Not really, anyway. He was probably just running from the flames and we got in the way. And he won't be the only animal trying to flee, so I need you to hand me the rest of those bandages, then stand guard while I patch this up. If anything comes through here that poses a threat, shoot it."

Her mind went blank—well, blanker, if that was even possible. Clearly, she wasn't cut out for this kind of life. She'd forgotten all about the gun tucked into her waistband and had turned to face whatever threat had come armed with nothing but a stick. A foolish and costly mistake.

"Because, believe it or not..." Caleb winced. "This is not our biggest concern right now."

"How can the threat of you bleeding to death not be our biggest concern?" She lifted a brow, and he couldn't help but grin at all the skepticism she managed to infuse into that one small gesture. She fumbled the bandages into his hands, added a roll of gauze, then glanced around as she jumped to her feet and pulled her gun from her waistband.

"Which brings me to the third thing." He wadded the bandages against the wound. Stars danced against a black background in his vision, and he clung precariously to consciousness.

Maintaining pressure against the wound, he started wrapping the gauze around his waist to hold the bandages in place until he could get them out of there—a task that had seemed much less daunting before he'd gone to scout ahead. He ignored the pain, had to if he was going to function well enough to get them out of there safely—or at all. "Someone basically set small brush fires in a circle surrounding our location."

"Why? Are they trying to force us to head toward them?"

He winced, partly from the pain, but also because there was no longer any doubt. Whoever was after Olivia didn't want to kidnap her for some reason; they wanted her dead. "Actually, they didn't leave an opening. They must have used an accelerant and set fires in a wide perimeter surrounding the crash site."

She paused for a moment to stare at him, then turned in a slow circle, eyes narrowed, assessing the situation as she kept an eye out for any more immediate threats.

He continued to treat his wound, giving her a moment to digest what he'd told her, allowing her to come to her own conclusion that there was no way out other than the one he was about to propose, which she was most likely not going to like. Who was he kidding? If her reaction to the small plane they'd flown back in was any indication, being hoisted into a helicopter from the ground was going to go over like a lead balloon.

Once he finished bandaging himself, he tucked everything away in the first aid kit and stuffed it into his backpack. Then, he shifted until he could lay a hand against the tree behind him, braced himself for the jolt of pain that was sure to come and tried to stand. His abdominal muscles tightened, the pain robbing him of breath.

Olivia was there in an instant, hooking his arm with her free hand to help him to his feet, holding her gun ready with the other.

Ranger pressed against his side, and Caleb leaned on him as little as possible to help regain his footing. When Ranger whimpered and licked his hand, Caleb petted his head. "You were a good boy, Ranger. I know you tried, and I'm glad Olivia stopped you."

She caught her lower lip between her teeth, clearly struggling beneath his weight. "You're sure I did the right thing? Because it doesn't feel like I did."

"Absolutely. The boar hit me on his way through simply because he was panicked and I was in his way, but he kept on going. If Ranger had attacked, it would have been a fight Ranger couldn't have won. And I wouldn't have been able to get a shot off with him in the way. Honestly, I'd have most likely ended up hurt anyway, because I would have had to intervene." He squinted against the searing sun and listened closely for the sound of Zac's chopper.

"So…" She followed his gaze, shielding her eyes from the sun with her gun hand. "Now what? How do we get out of here?"

He had to give her credit for her tenacity. They stood smack in the center of a ring of fire surrounded by enough dry, dead brush to fuel the flames even without an accelerant, and yet there was no indication that she was giving up hope.

He might have no idea who Olivia was, but he sure was learning a lot about her character. And everything she'd shown him so far proved his gut feeling that she was a good person who'd somehow gotten mixed up in something that was probably way out of her comfort zone. Either that, or he'd completely misjudged her. In survival situations, he trusted his instincts. They'd saved his life more than once. But when it came to people… Well, he trusted his instincts with Rachel and with Todd, a man who was supposed to have been his best friend, and look how that had turned out.

He took a step, testing his tolerance for the pain. Manageable. Okay, he could do this. "All right. We're going to have to walk about half a mile."

"I thought you said the nearest place they could land was about three miles from here?"

"Yeah. It is."

She stopped and faced him. "I don't understand."

He tried to come up with a way to ease the sting, but there was none, nor was there time. It would be better to just let her deal with the reality of what was to come. "They'll have to hoist us out."

Her expression remained neutral, and he found himself wishing she'd at least give some indication how she felt about that prospect. He had medication in the first aid kit that could help lessen her anxiety, but he was in no shape to get not only her and himself ready to lift up, but Ranger as well. He was going to need her help. He waited her out.

Finally, she nodded, wrapped an arm around his waist to take some of his weight, then started forward.

"So, that's it? You're good with that plan?" Better to know now if she was going to balk than to find out when she panicked at the last minute.

She shrugged and tucked the gun back into her waistband so she could grip the arm he slung around her shoulders for support. "Good's kind of a strong word."

He laughed—and instantly regretted it, as pain turned it to a wheeze. "You're all right. You know that?"

"Actually, I have no clue what I am. But for now, I'll just accept the compliment. Thank you."

Together, with Ranger at Caleb's heel, they inched slowly toward the small clearing he found when he and Ranger had scouted ahead.

She remained quiet, scowling, either from bearing his weight or some inner turmoil, before finally speaking. "Does it hurt when you talk?"

"No more than any other time. Why?"

"I don't know. I figured maybe since I can't remember anything about my past, or anything else I might be interested in talking about, you might tell me a little something about yourself. Who knows? Maybe it'll jog something in my memory—like the monkeys did earlier."

Caleb wasn't big on talking about himself, but she seemed so desperate to remember something—anything— that he was willing give it a shot. He eyed her warily, though. Somehow, he had a feeling she knew exactly what she was doing when she phrased the question as she had, as if he were helping her by talking about himself.

And something struck him with sudden clarity. He'd better watch his step around Olivia. He had a feeling she might be the one person who could worm her way past defenses he'd spent years erecting. "Sure. What would you like to know?"

"Are you married? Engaged? Do you have kids?" Her cheeks went bright red before she averted her gaze in the guise of scanning the sky, presumably for Zac's chopper. A chopper that couldn't get there fast enough in Caleb's mind. Not because he was frightened or injured. Not because he didn't want to spend time hiking in the forest with Olivia. But because she'd somehow managed to hit on every one of his sore points at once.

"I was married. Now I'm not." The words came out harsher than intended. But what was he supposed to say? That his wife had been cheating on him with his best friend? That she'd walked away and taken everything from him during what should have been the happiest moment of his life? He'd been so thrilled when he found out—

The familiar rage began as a spark in his gut, then flared through his chest and burned its way through him until it became so overwhelming it threatened to overpower his hard-won battle for control. And if that happened, he might lose his fight to keep from going after Todd Richardson.

Todd. Caleb's hands automatically fisted. His so-called best friend. Stupidly, Caleb hadn't realized how Todd was growing more and more jealous, more and more resentful of Caleb's professional and personal successes. He'd been determined to take what Caleb had. He'd admitted as much on the night he came to collect Rachel and all of her and the coming baby's belongings.

Caleb closed his eyes for a moment, willing the anger to subside, praying as he'd learned to do during his moments of solitude. *Please, God, give me the strength to wish only the best for them.*

"I'm sorry to hear that." Olivia gave his hand a squeeze, yanking him back to the present. Her eyes held kindness but no judgment and no sympathy, which would have stung even worse. "So, what about work? How long have you been with Jameson Investigations?"

He took a deep breath, grateful she let the matter drop without pushing for answers he wasn't ready to share, would most likely never be ready to share. Of course, now every answer that ran through his head was in terms of that moment in his life. He'd been so happy, so ready for their family to grow, so thrilled with the news that he and Rachel were going to have a child. If only the life he was imagining had been real. Instead, it had been nothing more than a mirage, shattered by her admission that their child wasn't his but Todd's. He started to speak, choked on the words, then cleared his throat. "Almost five years."

"It seems like you're really good at your job."

"I try." He was in too much pain to speak—physically and emotionally. But Olivia had no way of knowing that.

He studied her in his peripheral vision. What had she endured? He'd only known her for a day, and she'd already been through plenty that should have left her feeling sorry for herself. And yet, there was no indication that she did. Maybe he could learn a thing or two from Olivia.

The sound of an incoming chopper kept him from having to contemplate that thought any further. Probably for the best. "Have you ever been hoisted by…"

She glanced at him and lifted one brow, but there was humor in her expression.

"Right. Sorry. I forgot." He grinned, surprised he could under the circumstances.

"But if the fact that I'm absolutely terrified is any indication, probably not." That spark of humor faded, her eyes once more filling with fear.

"It's okay. I'll talk you through it." He ran a couple of scenarios in his head before settling on the one that would work best. "Okay, when they send down the strop, I'm going to secure you and let them hoist you up first."

She bit her lip and looked up as if envisioning what he'd explained. "What about you and Ranger?"

"I'll send Ranger right behind you, then I'll come up last."

She was shaking her head before he'd even finished his sentence. "Not happening."

"Excuse me?" His abdomen and hip throbbed. He could feel the blood running down his leg despite the bandage he'd managed to secure. And the thick smoke from the forest fires, which had accelerated wildly in the past few minutes, stung his eyes and clawed its way down the back of his throat. The last thing he needed right now was her giving him a hard time.

"Ranger can be lifted without you?"

He shrugged. "Sure. It won't be the first time we've had to be extracted from a difficult situation. Why?"

She studied Caleb, scanned the area, then her gaze fell on Ranger. "Send Ranger up first. Then show me how to secure myself, and you go up next."

"Absolutely not." No way was he leaving a civilian with no knowledge of the equipment alone in a burning forest.

"Well, you'd better figure something out quickly…" She planted her feet and propped her fists on her hips. "Because I've already told you I'm not leaving you down here alone."

"And I'm not leaving *you* alone. So, it seems we're at an impasse." The chopper moved closer. "There's no time to argue this. I know how to work the equipment, and I've trained for this, and I've done it before in an emergency situation."

"And you're bleeding profusely from a wound in your side." She gestured toward him, and he looked down at his blood-soaked shirt and khakis. The bandage was doing little to control the bleeding.

He pressed a hand against the wound.

"I'm not willing to risk you passing out down here while you're waiting your turn. Period. Can the two of us go up together?"

He nodded. They could, but he'd wanted to offer her some protection from the ground if their attackers showed up. Considering they'd ignited a circle around them, it was unlikely, but you could never be sure. "All right. We'll send Ranger up, then go up together."

"Fine. That'll work."

He just shook his head. "I'm glad you approve."

She shot him a mischievous grin, that humor winning

out over her fear again. Then she petted Ranger's head while they waited. She seemed to take comfort from the dog. He could certainly understand that, since Ranger had helped him through some extremely difficult moments.

After Caleb called Zac and relayed the situation and the extraction plan, they waited together while one of Zac's agents lowered a hoist for Ranger, each quietly contemplating their own thoughts. Caleb ran through their plan over and over, searching for every eventuality. Overall, it seemed like the best choice, but it wasn't ideal. He had no idea what thoughts might be plaguing Olivia. She was probably wondering how she'd gotten herself into this mess. Not that he could blame her.

Once he secured Ranger into the sling, he gave the signal for Mason Payne, one of the few agents Caleb felt comfortable entrusting Ranger with, to lift him up.

Olivia shielded her eyes with a hand, her gaze glued to Ranger. "You're sure he'll be okay?"

"It's not his favorite thing, but he'll be okay." Caleb kept an eye on his dog while he scanned the area—no easy feat.

"He's done this before?"

"Yeah. We got caught in a flood once and had to be airlifted out, and another time from the desert." He left out the part of the desert story where they'd been under heavy fire at the time. No need to scare her if it wasn't something she'd already thought of on her own.

The hoist lowered once again, and Caleb sagged a bit, leaning more of his weight onto Olivia as he shifted to grab the strop.

"You okay?" she asked, still looking up at the chopper.

"I'm fine." He secured the strop around Olivia, instructing her to lower her arms to keep the strop in position while he secured the straps, then tended to his own and checked the cable. Keeping her close, he signaled for Mason to begin hoisting them up.

Olivia pressed her lips together and closed her eyes as they lifted off. Her eyes flew open again as automatic gunfire tore through the foliage from the ground.

FIVE

A sharp sting ripped through Olivia's biceps. She automatically started to reach for her arm with her other hand, but Caleb gripped her wrist and held her firmly in place, then gestured toward the strop. Right, she had to keep her arms down. He'd told her that. She tried to ignore the burning sensation radiating through her arm, the pain surging through her body and the dizziness most likely caused by her head wound.

Above them, gunfire ripped through the afternoon in response to the shots from the ground. She didn't dare look down. Not after she risked a quick glance when they'd only been a few feet up and nearly gotten sick all over Caleb. Nor did she look above her to gauge the distance they still had to be lifted to the helicopter, especially since they seemed to have stopped moving upward as the helicopter banked and took them away from the fires and the gunshots.

The world spun around them as they hung suspended from the cable, the wind that tore between them keeping them from speaking. Okay, so she couldn't look up, she couldn't look down, and now she couldn't look straight ahead as they'd started to spin. And closing her eyes only made things worse.

But when she opened them, darkness encroached anyway, threatening to overwhelm her, to suck her into a deepening void. She had to fight it, had to remain conscious, couldn't leave Caleb responsible for both of them when he was already injured.

She inhaled deeply, squinted as tears streamed into her hairline and focused with a laser intensity on Caleb to keep from passing out.

She hadn't noticed before the dark green ring edging his hazel irises, or the fact that one eye had more blue than the other. Nor had she realized how attractive his scruffy five o'clock shadow was. And the fact that his ears stuck out just a bit too far amid his dark buzzed hair only added to his charm. Or perhaps she had noticed, considering each of those features stood out clear as day even though she could barely see through the tears the wind ripped from her eyes.

Yikes. Where had all that come from? For all she knew, she was a married woman with a houseful of kids. The thought left her unsettled. Could she have forgotten her own children? Her husband? Parents, siblings, friends? Great. Now she could either concentrate on the fact that she found Caleb to be attractive in addition to being brave, selfless and incredibly kind; she could wallow in self-pity because she had no memory of her life or anyone who might be important to her; or, she could live in the moment, dangling from a helicopter smack in the middle of an all-out gunfight. Some choices.

Then Caleb smiled at her.

Not the kind of smile someone offers when they know there's no way out but they're trying to keep your hopes up. His grin stretched from ear to ear while he gripped the cable, as if he were thoroughly enjoying the moment. She couldn't help but grin back at him.

When the bottom of the helicopter came into view, she was almost disappointed. Almost. Honestly, she couldn't wait to get her feet on something solid. At least the sounds of gunfire had finally stopped once they got out of range.

Caleb stretched his legs out and set his feet against the chopper, allowing an agent to pull Olivia onto the edge. Then, a large boom swung them inside, and Caleb reached behind him and slid the door closed.

Three men, two of whom had to set aside extremely large guns to help them, began to unhook Caleb and Olivia from the cable. She couldn't decide if the wall of men surrounding her made her feel safer or more threatened. Fear welled in her gut. Maybe she should have stayed in the forest, tried to find her own way out. Just because Caleb seemed to trust these men didn't mean she could. Because, truthfully, she was at their mercy. There was no escape from this chopper, no way to retreat from them if they intended any harm. The feeling of being trapped overwhelmed her.

Ranger danced back out of their way then squeezed between them to get next to Caleb the instant he spotted an opening. Surely, he wouldn't be so comfortable with them handling Caleb if he didn't trust them.

Tremors tore through Olivia's legs, and they threatened to buckle. She reached out blindly for something to grab onto. Her heart fluttered. Palpitations brought on by fear? A heart attack? It wouldn't surprise her, considering the ordeal she'd been through.

Caleb took her hand, his grip firm and strong amid utter

turmoil, a lifeline she could cling to as she struggled for balance, both physically and emotionally. He released her too soon as the agents separated them.

The pilot, who Caleb had told her was his boss, Zac Jameson, yelled something into his headset, and a tall man with dark hair and a killer smile gave him a thumbs-up. Then he motioned for Olivia to lift her arms so he could undo the strop.

Without thinking, she started to lift both arms over her head. Pain shot up to her shoulder and down to her fingers. She grabbed her biceps.

"No, don't touch it. Let Doc Rogers take a look," the guy yelled, then stepped back to allow another man to take his place. He waited for Caleb to pet Ranger, then led the big dog out of the way.

The doctor, a robust man with kind blue eyes, a headful of thick, wavy white hair and a neatly trimmed beard, smiled gently. He helped Olivia don a headset so she could hear him over the noise of the helicopter.

She'd never realized how noisy they would be. Then again, maybe she was a helicopter pilot. Who knew? She seemed to be more confused than ever.

"Hey, there, Olivia. I'm Dr. Rogers. Do you mind if I take a look at your arm?"

She let him guide her to a seat and help her buckle in. "I'm fine. Really, but Caleb was hurt badly when a boar attacked him. Please, tend to him first."

"Don't you worry about a thing. We'll take care of him. We knew what to expect from his last call, and I've already taken a cursory look, so Mason and Chase are getting him set up." He handed her wet wipes to clean the blood from her hand. "I'll just take a quick peek at your arm, and then I'll take care of Caleb."

After quickly wiping her hand clean, she held out her arm so he'd move on to Caleb more quickly. "Is Ranger okay?"

Ranger sat at attention, a sling of some sort wrapped around him and secured to a hook on the wall by a clip.

"Yup. He's good." He gave her arm a quick look. "It's just a graze. I'll—"

"Graze? Like, you mean a bullet wound? Like, I was shot?" She sucked in a deep breath and held it, embracing the ache in her lungs to keep from hyperventilating.

"Hey." Dr. Rogers gripped her chin and gently tipped her head until she looked him in the eye. "You're going to be fine."

Her teeth chattered, and she clamped them shut. When the doctor wrapped a blanket around her shoulders, she tucked it up around her chin and sank into the warmth, leaving her injured arm exposed.

He checked her vitals, then frowned. "Just give me your other arm so I can start an IV. I want to get you hydrated."

She hesitated for a moment. Trust him or not? She glanced at Caleb. He seemed to trust all of them implicitly, and Ranger looked on calmly. She slid the blanket down and extended her arm.

The doctor placed an oxygen tube beneath her nose, then warned of a small prick when he started the IV.

Shivers tore through her, and the instant he finished, she pulled the blanket tighter and cringed away from him.

"Listen to me, Olivia." He patted her hand beneath the blanket. "I know you've been through a lot."

A laugh threatened to bubble out. That might be the understatement of the century.

"And we're going to get you fixed up. I promise. But you're in shock, and I need you to try to relax."

She stared into his eyes, a soft blue that brought to mind a summer sky. He radiated kindness. She wanted so badly to trust him, to believe he was trying to take care of her, and she did, mostly. But she couldn't help the fear, the confusion, the desperation coursing through her. She was surrounded by strange men and, as well-intentioned as they seemed, she had no idea who she could trust. She needed to know who she was—and who she was running from. She needed to remember.

Dr. Rogers examined her injured arm, then the cut on her head. "Okay, I'm going to have Mason wrap your arm and rebandage your head wound. Once we reach the safe house, I'll clean and treat all of your injuries. Right now, I need you to work on calming yourself. Okay? You're safe here. I promise. No harm will come to you. Just breathe."

"Right. Yes. Breathe." She nodded, and a wave of dizziness took her. Battling the nausea, she forced herself to answer so the doctor would see to Caleb's wound. She was too unsteady, needed the firm feel of the ground stationary beneath her feet. "It's okay. I'm good. Thank you."

He studied her for a moment and then gave a small nod before shifting his attention to Caleb.

The same guy who'd pulled her into the chopper replaced Dr. Rogers. He squatted in front of her as the doctor moved on to Caleb and pulled bandages and gauze from a canvas bag.

She had to admit, the level of coordination between the three men was impressive. Even in the cramped quarters, they moved in unison, never seeming to get in each other's way, as if each change of position had been carefully choreographed. By the time the doctor moved the two feet to Caleb, another man had already taken his vitals and was in the process of starting an IV.

"Hi, Olivia. I'm Mason."

"Nice to meet you." Her response was automatic as she forced a smile, her attention on Caleb as the doctor spoke with him, then examined his wound. At least he was still conscious and talking. That had to be a good sign. Right?

"I'm just going to clean this out with a little antiseptic, then we'll bandage it up for now. Okay?"

She started to nod, then thought better of the idea. "Sure. Thank you."

While Mason tended to her arm, her focus remained on Caleb.

He lay on the floor of the cabin, his face pale, while the doctor administered something into the IV and rebandaged the wound. When Caleb laughed with the doctor and the other guy, she breathed a sigh of relief and slumped back in the seat. Surely, they wouldn't be laughing if he wasn't all right. And the laughter wasn't scary or mean-spirited. She could almost trust that none of the men on board posed a threat.

"How's that?" Mason patted her arm and sat back on his heels.

She pulled her attention from Caleb and tried to force a smile but failed miserably. "I'm fine. Thank you."

"Hey. Everything's going to be okay. Doc Rogers will take good care of him."

"Thank you. Would it be okay if I sit next to Ranger?" That would also put her a little closer to Caleb, where she could see if anything went wrong. She cut off the thought, desperately needing for him to be okay.

"Of course." Mason gave her a hand up and helped her buckle into the seat beside where Ranger sat.

When she scratched behind his ears, he dropped his head onto her lap, though his focus remained on Caleb. And with the big dog next to her, the knot of tension in her gut finally began to unravel. "He's going to be okay, boy."

Please, Lord, save him. Don't let him die because of me.

As they flew toward wherever they were taking her, Olivia remained quiet, thoughtful. Though the sound of the agents chattering through the headsets registered, she didn't pay attention to the logistics or their conversation. What did it matter anyway? It wasn't like she had a choice about what to do or where to go. She couldn't contribute anything worthwhile.

Someone was obviously after her, and she lacked the resources to keep herself safe. At least, she probably did. Who knew? It seemed she'd been taking a limo somewhere when they'd crashed. Maybe she had more resources than she thought.

All she knew for certain was that all of these people had risked their lives to save her. Caleb had risked his life and Ranger's to keep her safe, had been injured trying to do so. And she had no idea if she was worthy of their sacrifices.

What about the limo driver? Had he lost his life because of her? Had he sacrificed himself to save her? And what about the gun she found at the crash site? Had the weapon belonged to her? Firing it felt completely foreign, so she'd be surprised if that was the case. Did that mean it belonged to the driver? Had he been holding her at gunpoint, or had he been killed trying to protect her?

A stabbing pain in her temples cut her thoughts short. She needed answers. What had Caleb said? If she relaxed, maybe her memories would return? How had she known about the monkeys? Why had she been so comfortable in the Florida wilderness if she was from California?

She shook off the thoughts—again. She couldn't dwell on what she didn't know. All she could hope to do was focus on what she did know and what would come next. Her faith was strong. That much she did know. Would it be enough to see her through this?

She worked her way through one muscle at a time, feeling each ache and twinge as she struggled to ease the tension. Slowly, she began to relax. As she twined her fingers lazily through the fur on Ranger's head, her gaze inevitably returned to Caleb.

His complexion was paler than it had been, no doubt from blood loss. Dark circles ringed his eyes, but they still held a spark of humor when he smiled at her, easing the knot of tension in her gut even further. "Hey, you all right?" he asked.

Surely, he'd be okay. He had to be. She couldn't take it if something happened to him because of her. He'd shown such kindness, such compassion. A woman walking alone in the desert, injured, with no memory of who she was or how she'd gotten there could have ended so much differently. And this time, the smile she returned was genuine. "Well, I may not know much about myself, other than I apparently have monkey trivia mastered. But after that ordeal, I can tell you with one hundred percent certainty, I am not an adventurous woman."

Caleb's laughter touched something in her, allowing her to shake off her fears. Well, some of them, anyway. She'd get through this. Probably. But what would she find out about herself along the way?

When Zac finally set the helicopter down on a helipad, she pulled her mind away from that precipice. It would be too easy to tip over the edge into despair. For now, she needed to stay positive. When she least expected it in the forest, a memory had returned to her. At least that gave her hope that the rest of her memories were still there, locked up in some dark corner.

Now, if she could just find the key to accessing them.

Once Doc Rogers had finished stitching Caleb up, running a round of IV antibiotics and scolding him for getting gouged, he patted Caleb's knee where he sat on an examination table in a makeshift clinic in one of the four bedrooms in the safe house Zac had procured. "One of these days, you guys are going to stop getting yourselves into trouble, and I'm going to retire and go fishing all day long."

Caleb grinned. The old man had been saying that since Caleb had met him. "I wouldn't count on that, Doc. Besides, who are you kidding? You'd be bored within two hours, tops."

"Yeah, yeah." He stepped back. "Just make sure you keep this clean and change the bandages. Angela already picked up your antibiotic prescription. Take them as directed, and you should be good as new in no time."

"Sure thing. Can I go now?" He didn't want to admit, even to himself, maybe especially to himself, how anxious he was to see Olivia. Although the doc had assured him— multiple times—that she was okay, he needed to see her for himself. He hadn't realized she'd been shot until Dr.

Rogers had mentioned it while stitching him up, and he'd thought of nothing else since.

"Yeah. Just try to take it easy. I don't want you messing up my beautiful sutures."

"Thank you, Doc. I promise, I'll do my best." He laughed, hopped off the table and winced at the twinge of pain. Then he ignored it. It wasn't the worst pain he'd ever suffered.

The doctor had been blessed with an easy smile and kind eyes that could put anyone at ease. And his eyes held a bit of a twinkle when he said, "She's in the living room with Angela."

"Who is?"

Doc Rogers just laughed and shook his head.

So much for Caleb's poker face. It didn't matter, though. Any interest he might feel toward Olivia was strictly professional. He'd agreed to protect her, and he took that commitment seriously. Especially after his recent failure.

"And after you've checked in on her and Ranger, there's clean clothes in the last bedroom on the right."

"Thanks again, Doc." Caleb took his time walking to the living room, partly in deference to the wound that still throbbed but mostly because he needed a moment to collect himself. He'd been shot at before, even while dangling defenseless from a chopper, but he'd never known fear like he had when Olivia had been the one in the crosshairs. What was it that made her so different from others he'd protected over the years? Compassion for her situation? Waking up alone, injured and unable to remember anything about yourself or your past had to be terrifying. And yet, she'd shown nothing but courage and consideration for others since he'd met her. If nothing else, she definitely intrigued him.

He found her in the living room, sitting on the floor in the far corner with her legs stretched out in front of her and her head tilted back against the wall, eyes closed. Her hair hung in long waves around her shoulders. She'd cleaned up and changed into black leggings and an oversize olive green sweatshirt that made her appear even more petite, more fragile. Ranger lay beside Olivia with his head in her lap, and she absently stroked his fur.

Caleb crossed the room to them quietly, started to speak, then had to clear his throat when whatever words he might have said got caught there.

Ranger's head popped up, and he scrambled to his feet and shot toward Caleb.

Caleb opened his arms to the big dog, petting him as Ranger squirmed and twirled, licking Caleb's hands and face. He couldn't help but laugh. "I'm happy to see you, too, Ranger."

When he looked up from Ranger, Olivia smiled at him. "It's good to see you up and around. Are you all right?"

"I'm good, thanks. The doc fixed me all up and assures me I'll be good as new in no time. I'm sorry, though. I didn't mean to intrude on your moment of peace." And with that, he turned tongue-tied, unable to decide exactly what he could say to her.

"That's okay. I have a feeling it was about to be interrupted anyway." She gestured past him.

Angela Ryan, a tall, handsome woman with sharp, angular features, rich umber skin and closely cropped black hair, strode toward them, interrupting what would probably have stretched into an awkward silence.

Caleb reached out a hand and helped Olivia up, then gestured for her to sit in an armchair and took the one opposite her. Ranger sat between them. His ears tipped forward as he went on alert at Angela's approach. Not that he didn't know Angela—he did—but her presence was often followed by work mode.

"I'm sorry, Olivia, but we couldn't find a match for your fingerprints."

"Great." Olivia shoved her hands through her hair and squeezed the strands, then blew out a frustrated breath and let them drop into her lap. "So, where does that leave us?"

"Well, look on the bright side." Caleb gave her arm an affectionate nudge. "At least, you're not a criminal."

"Or maybe I am, and I've never gotten caught because I'm just that good." She winked at him.

And something in his belly flipped over—probably residual motion sickness from their ordeal. Not that he'd ever been prone before, but there was always a first time. Maybe he'd ask the doc for some Dramamine.

"She's got you there." Angela laughed, then gestured toward the kitchen. "My computer is set up on the island in the kitchen, Olivia. When you're ready, if you want to meet me there, I'm about to examine the flash drive you gave me. Maybe it'll tell us something. And, if it's okay with you, I'd like to take your picture and run it through a facial recognition program."

Olivia caught her lower lip between her teeth and nodded slowly. Her eyes suddenly went wide, and she jumped up. "Come with me."

Since she didn't specify who she meant, Caleb glanced at Angela. She shrugged and followed Olivia down the hallway, Caleb and Ranger close on her heels.

In one of the bedrooms, Olivia opened a dresser drawer, pulled out the picture of the woman she'd shown Caleb earlier and held it out to Angela. "Can you run this through facial recognition, too, and find out who she is?"

Angela studied the photo, then turned it over and checked the back for markings. "Where'd you get this from?"

"It was in my pocket with the flash drive when I woke in the burning limo." Olivia narrowed her eyes as she studied the picture with Angela. "I have no idea who she is or why I'd be carrying her picture with me."

"Hmm. Interesting. And that was all you had on you? The flash drive and this photo?"

"Yup. That's it. And I picked up a handgun at the scene, but I'm not sure that was mine." She spared Caleb a quick glance.

"All righty, then, let's see what we can find out." Angela turned and started down the hallway, the *click, click, click* of her heels and Ranger's claws against the hardwood floor the only sounds.

When Angela sat in front of her laptop at the kitchen island, Caleb pulled out a stool and gestured for Olivia to sit beside her. He sat on Angela's other side so he'd be able to see the computer screen. Even if he wanted to sit beside Olivia. That was his protective instinct. It had nothing to do with the citrusy scent from Olivia's freshly washed hair or the fact that he wanted to put his arm around her and reassure her that he would keep her safe. How could he do so when he had no idea what they were up against or if he'd be able to follow through on that promise?

Thankfully, Angela moved quickly, and a moment later row after row of code began popping up on the screen.

He leaned closer from one side as Olivia did so from the other side, bringing them practically ear to ear. So much for putting a little distance between them. "What are we looking at?"

Angela shrugged and looked to Olivia. "The patterns and format make me think some sort of financial records, but they're coded. Do you know how to decipher the code, Olivia?"

She bit her lip and shook her head slowly, her eyes glued to the screen. "I... I don't know."

"Are you sure?" Caleb prodded at her hesitation.

"It doesn't make sense." After studying the code for a few minutes, she sat back and blew out a breath, ruffling a few strands of hair that had fallen in front of her face. "I feel like I *should* know how to decode it, like there's something familiar here, but my mind is just a total blank."

Caleb stood and moved behind her, rested a hand on her shoulder. "It'll be okay. I'm sure everything will come back to you, especially since you recognize that you should know this. It's only a matter of time."

"Yeah. Too bad we don't have time, considering another attack could come at any moment." She shook her head, then lowered her face into her hands.

At a loss as to what he could do to help, Caleb gave up and returned to his seat. "What about the photo? The woman resembles Olivia enough that they could be related. Maybe if we can identify her, it will lead us to a clue about Olivia's identity."

"Sure." Angela opened a new window, then took the photo to the scanner.

"Hey. Olivia." Caleb expected to find her expression defeated, but when she looked at him, he saw only determination. "We'll figure this out. You have my whole team behind you now. And when Zac and Angela set their minds to something, they usually figure it out."

"I don't know how I can ever thank you, Caleb. When I think about what could have happened to me out in that desert…"

"Hey." He started to reach for her hand, then thought better of the idea and let his own drop. This woman's life was in enough turmoil. The last thing he wanted was to give her the impression he was interested in anything other than helping her out of this jam. He'd been down that road already, and it had led to nothing but heartbreak. He had no intention of ever following that path again. "There's no sense thinking about what-ifs. Let's just concentrate on figuring out who you are and then take it from there. I firmly believe I was led to find you, so I have to believe we'll figure this out as well."

She nodded and offered the shaky smile he'd come to enjoy coaxing from her. "Thanks."

"You bet."

Angela returned a moment later with her cell phone and took a picture of Olivia. "This could take a little while. Mason and Chase just set sandwiches out on the dining room table. Why don't you guys grab something to eat, and I'll let you know what I come up with?"

"Thank you," Olivia called after her as Angela hurried away. Then she turned to Caleb. "Now what?"

"Now we follow Angela's advice and get something to eat while we wait to see what she can come up with."

She quirked a brow at him. "And pray no one finds us in the meantime?"

He shrugged and gestured for her to precede him toward the dining room. "Sometimes that's all we can do."

"I guess. But somehow, I don't think patience is my strong suit."

He couldn't help but laugh. He had a feeling Olivia knew herself better than she realized.

It seemed Chase and Mason had already taken pieces of the four-foot Italian gyro and disappeared, since they were on guard duty at the moment. Angela's occasional frustrated muttering reached them from the kitchen. Zac stood in the living room, looking out the window and tapping a pen against the sill while he spoke in a hushed voice on the phone, and Doc Rogers had gone to get some medical equipment.

That left Caleb and Olivia alone at the dining room table once they'd filled their plates with Ranger lying beside him. "Can I get you something to drink?" Caleb asked. "A bottle of water or soda? Tea, coffee?"

"Water would be fine, thank you."

He grabbed a couple of bottles from the fridge, checked in on Angela's lack of progress, then returned to Olivia.

She pushed potato salad around her plate with her fork. "Well, since I can't remember anything about myself that might make for interesting small talk, and it appears you're stuck with me for the foreseeable future, how about telling me a little more about you?"

"There's not much to tell, really." He took a bite of his sandwich and chewed slowly, giving himself time to decide what he could tell her without spiraling down the rabbit hole he had the last time she asked.

"Do you always hang out in remote deserts waiting to rescue damsels in distress?" Olivia asked.

"More often than you'd think, really. I mean…the hanging out in remote areas part, not the rescuing damsels part. I…uh…"

Her laughter was worth his moment of discomfort.

"What I mean to say is, I often go off the grid after a particularly difficult case."

"And you'd just finished one when you came across me?" She took a bite of her sandwich.

Caleb might have balked at sharing any of his story, but she seemed interested, and she'd finally started to eat something rather than chase it around her plate with a fork, so he opened up a little. "My last case ended badly. I was charged with protecting a couple scheduled to testify at a trial for a gang member accused of murder. I had to make a court appearance, so another Jameson Investigations agent was called in to take my place."

She watched him, seemed to gauge his need to tell his story at his own pace, in his own way. She ate slowly, giving him time to find the words to convey the pain he'd suffered, the heartache that still plagued him.

He set down his fork and fisted his hands on the table. "While I was gone, someone blew up the entire building, killing the agent, the couple and everyone else who'd been inside."

"Oh, no, Caleb." She reached across the table and laid her hand over his. "I'm so sorry. I can't imagine how awful that must have been."

He nodded, surprised he'd shared that much, even more surprised he felt as if a very small portion of the burden had been lifted in the telling. He'd shoulder that responsibility forever—even though he'd had no choice but to attend and testify at the trial and hadn't been the one to choose the agent who took his place. No matter how many times Zac drilled those two facts into his head, it never seemed to alleviate any of his guilt. "I'll always wonder if having Ranger there would have made a difference, if he'd have detected the bomb before it went off."

"If he had," she said softly, "would you have had time to evacuate everyone?"

He shrugged. It was a question he'd asked himself a million times. "There's no way to know."

She squeezed his hand, seeming to know there was nothing she could say to help. But that silent offer of support meant more to him than any words she might have offered.

"Anyway, that's the story of what I was doing in the desert when I found you."

"Well, for what it's worth, I'm glad you were the one to find me. Thank you."

He nodded. It was worth more than she realized.

She sipped her water, then recapped the bottle and set it aside. "I don't know how you go back to it after things go so wrong."

"Because more often, things go right. My goal in life is to save as many people as possible." He clamped his mouth shut. He hadn't meant to let that slip, but Olivia was so easy to talk to. He'd do well to keep his guard up around her for sure. And the sudden realization that she might be more dangerous than the killers on their heels took hold. Because he feared she might be the one person who could force her way past the walls he'd so painstakingly erected around his heart after losing Rachel.

Thankfully, Angela walked in just then and interrupted.

Good thing, too, or he might have blurted out his whole painful past. "It's a pleasure to meet you, Olivia Delaney."

Olivia went perfectly still. "Are you sure?"

"Absolutely. We just got a positive ID. You work for Delaney Investments, your late father's company. You own approximately twenty-four percent of the company, as does your sister, Amy, while your brother, Tristan, owns the majority fifty-two percent." She paused, studying Olivia. If she was waiting for a reaction, one wasn't forthcoming. Olivia's neutral expression appeared etched in stone. "You have an address in California, but you also have a small cabin in your name here in Florida."

She shot to her feet. "I have to go there."

"Why? Do you remember it?"

"No. Not at all." And yet, something about the humid air, the smell of the vegetation in the forest, the billowing clouds amid the canvas of blue sky, had seemed more familiar to her than anything in the California desert. "But maybe something will come back to me if I see it."

An agent walked in and handed Angela a folder. She spoke with him in hushed tones as she opened it and perused the contents.

Olivia's attention was riveted on Caleb.

She might be right. Maybe it would help for her to see familiar surroundings, but still... "I can't take you to the cabin. You having a place here... It makes more sense how your attackers found us. They obviously expected you'd run to Florida."

He paused as that sank in. If her memory had really failed her, why would she have been so willing to return to Florida? He tried to think back to their conversation in the desert, when he'd offered to fly her across the country.

She hadn't remembered anything up until that point, but suddenly she'd been so eager to fly off with him. Could he have misjudged her? Could the amnesia be a scam? Maybe she'd simply claimed to have no memory so she wouldn't have to answer questions, so he'd agree to help her avoid the police. Had her goal been to get to her cabin all along? For what purpose?

His heart sank. Something about her had made him trust her more than he should have. He should have known better, had learned the hard way to trust no one. So, what was different about Olivia Delaney? Was it truly divine grace that led him to her in the California desert, when she needed to be in Florida, where Zac's headquarters was co-incidentally based? Or had Olivia pulled the wool over his eyes? It all came down to one thing—why had he wanted to believe in her?

"I have to go there, Caleb." Olivia stood her ground, rousing his suspicions even further. "You don't have to come with me. In fact, it's probably better if you don't. I've already put everyone in enough danger."

"You're not going anywhere alone." Not even if she was lying to him. He may be willing to see her in prison if she'd done something illegal, though the thought caused bile to burn up the back of his throat, but he didn't want to see her get killed. And whatever she might have done couldn't possibly warrant a death sentence. Besides, whatever she was up to, he needed to see it through. If not for her sake, then for his own. What was so important she had to return to her cabin despite the fact that it was a huge security risk?

He sighed, knowing he was going to give in. Were his instincts begging him to believe her or warning him to back off? He had no idea. Now, it seemed, he couldn't even trust himself.

"Can I please borrow a car? Or now that we know who I am, maybe I can access my bank accounts and rent one—"

"Okay." He held his hands up, desperately needing a moment to make sense of all of this. "Enough. You're not going anywhere alone. You asked me to protect you. Remember?"

She folded her arms in a defiant gesture. "I remember just fine."

All right, so the word had come out a bit more sarcastically than he intended. It didn't mean he was going to throw her to the wolves. "I'll agree to take you, but only if we go later, near dark, after the doc finishes running whatever tests he deems necessary to diagnose the cause of your amnesia."

She seemed to chew on that for a moment, then let her arms drop. "Fine. Thank you."

He simply nodded, too physically and mentally exhausted to continue the argument. If she was telling the truth, which he would assume she was for now, a quick peek at the life she couldn't remember might give her a chance to heal.

Angela cleared her throat. "Now that you two have finished bickering…"

A smile played at the corners of Olivia's mouth, and she lowered her gaze.

"Olivia, Doc Rogers has returned and has everything set up in the back bedroom to begin running tests, so if you'll follow me—"

"I need to know what else you've found out about me. Please."

Angela offered a reassuring smile. "Of course you do, and while Doc's running his tests, we'll come to you with everything as we find it out. Okay?"

"All right. Thank you."

"Before we start, though, you should also know that you've been reported missing by your brother and are presumed dead. And…" Her gaze skipped to Caleb. She offered an apologetic smile before returning her attention to Olivia. "Your fiancé has offered a hefty reward for any information on your whereabouts, whether or not you survived."

Caleb's mind raced. Her fiancé?

Olivia went completely still. She appeared to be shocked into silence as she allowed Angela to steer her into the exam room.

He held his breath and waited until Angela pulled the door shut behind her, then pounced. "What do you mean, fiancé?"

Angela leafed through the pages in the folder, then handed him a photo. "Lloyd Wellington. He works for Delaney Investments."

He stared at the headshot. The guy was handsome, he had to admit, though in a sleazy, gangster sort of way. Caleb caught himself and massaged the bridge of his nose. How could he judge a man from a photo? And why did he feel it was his right to judge him at all? He needed to get a grip on his out-of-control emotions, needed to change tack. "You said she owns a percentage of the company?"

"Yes. Twenty-four percent, according to public records, though she's only worked there for a bit over a year. On paper, anyway. And not in management, she's a junior analyst."

That was strange. "Why was she working an entry-level position?"

Angela shrugged. "I don't know, she graduated college, then seemed to go off grid for a good five years, then showed up in California just after her father passed away. We'll dig deeper, but that's all we have so far."

So what had she been doing between college and showing up at Delaney Investments?

"We've collected pictures of Delaney Investments, the house she owns in California and a few family members. I figured we could show them to her after Doc's done running the tests."

"No time like the present." Keeping Lloyd's photo in his hand, he knocked then shoved the door open and gestured for Angela to precede him.

Having just completed the bloodwork, Doc was setting up for the next test, an EEG it seemed. "Can you lie down, please, Olivia?"

She started to roll her sleeve down.

"Doc, can you give us one minute? We have some photos for her to look at."

"Sure. I'll be here all day."

Angela approached Olivia and handed her a picture of an office building. "This is your family's company, where you've worked as an analyst for the past year. Do you recognize it?"

She took the picture from Angela, studied it and frowned. "No. Not at all."

"That's okay, dear." Doc Rogers patted her hand. "We'll figure it out."

She nodded, sniffed and took the next photo from Angela. "What's this?"

"A picture of your house in California. You bought it just over a year ago, when you returned to California after your father's death."

Tears dripped onto the photo. Because she remembered her father or because she didn't? She shook her head and handed the picture back to Angela.

Next Angela handed her a photo of Tristan Delaney. "You have two half siblings. You had a photo of Amy with you. This is your half brother, Tristan. Take your time. Does he look at all familiar?"

She barely looked at it before shaking her head. "Can we do this later, please?"

"Of course." Angela tucked the photos back into the folder and started to back away.

"Just one more for now." Caleb stepped in, because he wasn't leaving without gauging her reaction to the photo of her fiancé. He didn't wait for an answer, just held the photo out to her without telling her who it was and kept his gaze glued to her expression.

When she glanced at the picture, something flared in her eyes, only for an instant before she shut it down. But it wasn't recognition. If he wasn't mistaken, it was fear. Why would Olivia be frightened of the man she was supposed to marry?

SIX

Fiancé? She glanced again at her bare left hand, not even a tan line where a ring might once have been. Angela's report had hit Olivia like a sucker punch. She was still trying to wrap her head around the fact that she was engaged to someone—someone she had absolutely no memory of. Not that she hadn't considered the idea that she might be involved with someone—she had. But her immediate reaction to Angela's words had been disappointment, and that confused her as much as everything else that had gone on over the past couple of days.

Even hours later, just the thought had her breaking out in a cold sweat. A tremor ran through her. If she was planning to marry someone, she must be in love with him. Right? So, why had her first reaction to seeing his photo been fear?

Her brother's image had elicited a similar reaction. Why would she feel so uneasy about a brother she couldn't even remember? Why would she be frightened of her own fiancé? None of it made any sense. Did the fact that he'd offered a large reward mean he was wealthy? Was it his limo she'd been riding in when they crashed?

An instant of terror washed over her at the memory of the man killed in the crash. But if her fiancé was offering a reward, he had to still be alive. So who had been killed? Her driver?

"You okay?" Caleb had been unusually quiet in the hours since they'd found out who Olivia was.

Granted, they hadn't had much time together before the drive out to the cabin, since Dr. Rogers had insisted on running so many tests to look for the cause of Olivia's amnesia. When she still refused to go to the hospital, Zac had somehow managed to procure a portable CT scanner and MRI machine, along with technicians to run the tests. They'd also done an EEG and bloodwork.

While she spent the majority of the day with the doctor, getting poked and prodded, Caleb had worked with Angela and the others to investigate Olivia's past. But he hadn't spoken much to Olivia after showing her Lloyd's photo.

"I'm fine. Thank you." What else could she say? At least, now she knew who she was. Olivia Delaney. A name that may as well belong to a stranger for all the awareness it evoked. The doctor had assured her he was only testing out of an abundance of caution, and he seemed fairly certain her memory loss was the result of some kind of trauma— her brain's way of trying to protect her from psychological harm. But what could have happened to her that was so bad she'd refused to remember? And if it was her own mind causing the problem, why couldn't she just fight it and bring the memories back? Then again, if it was that bad, maybe she didn't want to remember. Maybe that was the problem.

The hum of the tires against the pavement threatened to deafen her in the silence.

"Thank you for agreeing to take me to the cabin. I know you're concerned it's not the right thing to do."

Caleb had voiced his opinion—loudly and repeatedly. An opinion she would share, if she allowed herself to think about it. But she had to see the cabin that might be her... hers. She couldn't bring herself to think of the small cabin Angela had found on the outskirts of the forest as home. She had no idea if she'd ever lived there or if it was a vacation home.

Did it even belong to her? Maybe her fiancé, Lloyd Wellington according to Angela, had bought the cabin in her name. Or perhaps her brother, Tristan, had purchased the cabin. From what Angela could dig up, it seemed he ran the empire left by their father after he'd passed away.

Something tugged at her heart—the first sign of any kind of emotional reaction to these strangers who were supposed to be her family. Had she and her father been close?

"Stop trying so hard. You're going to hurt yourself."

"Huh?" Her gaze jerked to Caleb.

He frowned, then reached out and smoothed a finger across the bridge of her nose. He cradled her cheek for a moment, then let his hand drop. "You're thinking so hard you're giving yourself wrinkles."

She forced a smile. "Sorry. I know I'm not the best company right now."

"Hey." He returned his hand to the wheel of the black SUV Zac had lent them. "No worries. I'm not looking for you to entertain me. I just feel..."

She studied him, waiting when he hesitated, as if he'd lost track of what he started to say.

"I'm just sorry you're going through all of this, and I'll be here for you for as long as you need me."

Ranger poked his head between the front seats from

where he sat in the back and barked once, then licked her cheek.

"Ugh, Ranger, really?" She wiped her cheek, but this time her smile and her laughter were genuine. "Thank you, Caleb. You, too, Ranger."

"You'll get through this, Olivia, even if it doesn't seem like it right now."

"How do you do that?"

"Do what?"

"Stay so positive. Even after everything you've been through recently." When Ranger tilted his big head onto her shoulder, she leaned against him, his fur tickling her cheek. She reached around to hug him and stroked his flank.

Caleb shifted in his seat, and she sensed he'd probably endured more tragedy than he told her about. "I have to remind myself all the time that forgiveness is not just for others. We have to learn how to forgive ourselves, too. Since there's no way to turn back time, all we can do is live with our mistakes every day and try to do better the next time around. Who knows? Maybe living with the guilt is part of our penance."

"I don't believe that, Caleb. God forgives all of our sins if we repent, so who are we not to forgive ourselves?" Of course, that was easy for her to say, considering she had no knowledge of any of her past transgressions.

He shrugged. "I guess it's a lesson I'm still learning."

"Which explains the retreats into solitude." Where he probably spent most of his time beating himself up over his failures.

"Something like that." He gestured ahead of them. "We're going to make a right into the forest in two miles. Once we do, we'll be on a dirt road leading deeper into the woods, and there will be no easy way to turn around if we're attacked. Are you sure about this?"

Was she? She had no idea.

But she did know she had to see the cabin. One, to see if it prodded her memory. And two, to search for some clue as to why someone was trying to kill her, since nothing Angela had turned up gave any indication she was in trouble. According to all of the research done by Zac's team, Olivia lived in California and worked as an analyst in her family's investment firm. She didn't use social media, as far as anyone could tell. She'd never been in trouble with the law. And she had little to no digital imprint except a small bio on the firm's website saying she'd graduated from a college in Florida with a double major in business and computer science and a minor in art. After an extended stay, she'd returned home to California to take her place in the company business.

"I'm sure. I'm sorry, Caleb. I don't want to put you or Ranger at risk again, but I have to know why someone is after me. And why I was carrying that picture of my sister around." A picture in which she looked so sad? The woman in the photo had been identified as Olivia's older half sister and a junior partner at Delaney Investments. So, why didn't the sight of her evoke the same kind of gut fear her brother and fiancé's photos had? And why was Olivia an entry-level analyst when she also technically owned a portion of the company her brother and sister were currently running?

A dull throb started at her temples. There were too many questions she needed answers to. "Why don't you drop me off at the end of the dirt road, and I'll walk in myself? Angela gave me a cell phone to use and programmed in your number, so I can call you when I'm done, and you can come back and pick me up."

His jaw clenched. "Not happening, so don't even bother asking again. Until this is over, you're stuck with me."

"And after it's over?" She tried to bite back the words the instant they left her lips, but it was too late. She didn't know why she said it, or even why she'd thought it when she was obviously set to marry someone else. She had no interest in Caleb as anything other than a friend, but the thought of him and Ranger walking away and never looking back gave her a sinking feeling she didn't dare examine too closely. "What I mean is, when this is all said and done, I'd like to remain friends, maybe keep in touch."

He smiled. "I'd like that, too."

With that, they both fell silent as Caleb turned onto the narrow, rutted dirt road and started into the forest. The trail, barely wide enough for the SUV, weaved between giant, moss-covered oaks and beautiful, majestic pine trees. Algae-covered water-filled ditches ran along either side of the road. Caleb was right about one thing— a U-turn and a hasty retreat were definitely off the table.

She sat up straighter, taking in her surroundings as they drove deeper into the forest. Was this where she'd lived in the years before she returned to California? Had she been here alone? She couldn't imagine it, though there was an odd sense of familiarity, of comfort, unlike the emptiness that had filled her when looking at the picture of the California house that was supposedly her home.

A few minutes later, when the dirt path finally opened up into a small clearing and Caleb stopped in front of a rustic-looking, wood-plank cabin, she hopped out of the car.

She turned in a slow circle, taking in what appeared

to be a natural clearing in the woods. The soft, warm, spicy-sweet scent of local plants teased her senses as did the more pungent odor of those that had begun to decay. A hawk screeched as it soared overhead, its wings spread majestically.

The cabin stood on a shore, surrounded by prehistoric-looking forest and backed by swamplands. A boardwalk ran from the back door to a wooden dock, and she knew without a doubt how the third board from the end would squeak and give a little when you stepped on it. She closed her eyes for a moment and immersed herself in her surroundings. Although nothing jogged her memory, a sense of peace settled over her. "I'd like to look inside."

"Okay." Caleb seemed content to hang back and let her take the lead. With his head on a constant swivel, he surveyed their surroundings as she climbed the two steps to the wraparound porch. Without thinking, she picked up a rock from a long planter centered below the front window and overflowing with hibiscus plants in a variety of colors. She slid the false bottom open and shook a key out into her hand.

Caleb propped his hands on his hips, narrowed his eyes and watched her from the front step, but he did nothing to interfere, simply left her to figure this out on her own.

Ranger stood beside him, head tilted, studying her just as intently.

How had she known where the key was? Like the monkey trivia and the squeak of the boardwalk, it just seemed to be random knowledge that came to her without any awareness of how or why she knew what she did. Maybe Caleb was right, and her memory would return if she just tried to relax.

She let it go for now. If she got too hung up on that thought, she might miss something important. She'd have time later, once they were back at the safe house, to decipher the meaning of whatever information they uncovered. For now, she'd have to content herself with seeing what she could find and cataloguing it for further examination.

She unlocked the front door and pushed it open. Dust motes floated in the rays of the setting sun that pierced the back windows. A pair of sandhill cranes launched themselves into the air and soared deeper into the swamp.

Caleb moved past her, Ranger beside him wearing his work vest, as they did a quick reconnaissance of the two-bedroom cabin. "It doesn't look like anyone's been here, but we should move quickly. It'll be getting dark soon."

It was probably all the prodding he'd do, but still, she didn't need the reminder that the sun was setting on another day with no memories.

The rustic kitchen boasted old-fashioned wood cabinets and a hunter-green countertop. A rack filled with copper pots hung above a large center island, and a breakfast bar separated the space from a living room with a comfy-looking sectional and a massive stone fireplace bracketed by bookshelves that took up an entire wall.

The ball of tension that had been building inside her since the accident, and maybe even before that—who knew?—started to unravel. She ran her fingers along the spines of a few books, some of which bore enough creases to imply they were very well read. She supposed that might be one up-side of amnesia. She could reread all her favorite books, and it would be like reading them for the first time. Provided, of course, these were her books. What if she rented the cabin to someone else, and she was nothing more than a trespasser?

But would a stranger keep a photo of her on the mantel? Probably not. She lifted the frame and studied the image. It showed her with a brilliant smile, joy emanating from her even in the still photo. She stood on the dock out back, her head tilted against an elderly man's shoulder, his arm slung protectively around her.

Her breathing hitched, not for any memory of the father she'd lost, but at the apparent love between the two of them that she couldn't remember. She set the photo back on the mantel and swiped the tears rolling down her cheeks.

And then Caleb was there. He pulled her into his embrace, gently cradled her head, then smoothed his hand over her hair. "It's going to be okay, Olivia. I'm sure your memories will come back in time. Doc Rogers said it wasn't unusual to lose your memory after a traumatic experience and that you just need to be patient with yourself and give it time."

She nodded against him and surrendered herself for just one moment, allowing herself to accept the comfort he offered, reveling in the feeling of safety being cocooned in his arms evoked.

And then she stepped back. Not that it was wrong to take comfort from a friend, and not that Caleb had insinuated he was interested in anything other than friendship, but because in her heart, she wished they'd met under different circumstances or, at least, that she wasn't engaged to someone else. And that wasn't fair to anyone involved. *Forgive me, God. And thank you for sending Caleb to rescue me.*

She'd do well to remember that that was all he was—her rescuer and, perhaps, her friend.

He stuffed his hands into his pockets and rocked back onto his heels. "Do you want to take the photo with you?"

Did she? She didn't know. It seemed right just where it was. The tears started up again.

"Hey. Don't worry. It's clear how much the two of you loved each other. I'm sure the memories will all come back to you in time."

"Yeah." She sniffed, grabbing hold of the anger welling within her at her weakness. It was easier to deal with than the fear, the sadness, the grief. "And when they do, will it be like losing him all over again?"

He opened his mouth as if to speak, then seemed to think better of it and snapped it closed again.

She turned away from the photo and Caleb and wandered down a short hallway. A bathroom stood at the end, surprisingly large. Though rustic in design, it contained a large claw-foot tub and an oversize shower stall with multiple showerheads. If the vast variety of bath balls arranged in several baskets on the shelf beside the tub and the assortment of well-burned candles alongside them were any indication, she enjoyed pampering herself. Too bad it wasn't a luxury she could afford right now.

She checked the bedroom to her left from the doorway, since the door stood open. A patchwork quilt in a variety of earth tones covered a queen-size bed with a cedar chest at its foot. A rocking chair sat in one corner, turned to face the view of the swamp from the back window, and an assortment of oil paintings filled the walls, all some variation of the Florida wilderness. Her gaze caught on the painting above the bed, the monkeys rolling, swinging and playing amid the cypress trees in the lake.

Since she wasn't ready to face any more heartbreak, she

decided to save that room for later. Instead, she turned to the closed door opposite her bedroom and pushed it open. She took one step inside and stopped dead in her tracks. A scarred countertop ran the entire length of one wall. Tubes of oil paints were neatly arranged in cubbies along the back, paintbrush holders filled to capacity stood along-side them, and several easels dotted the room. A rack filled with blank canvases took up one corner.

But her attention fell on the work in progress standing on an easel beside the window. It was a half-finished paint-ing of the swamp. On closer inspection, she found a spot-ted bobcat peering from between a grouping of fan palms. Something in her stirred, and she knew she'd painted the picture from a sighting she'd had while hiking in the for-est. Another canvas sat on the counter, a finished swamp scene that bore the signature Olivia Malcolm. Malcolm—her father's name. A pseudonym she used for her artwork? But why?

The memory teased her. It was there—she knew it. Now, if she could only reach out and grab hold. She might be an analyst by trade, but her passion was art.

Ranger barked twice, then went on alert.

Olivia whirled toward Caleb even as he grabbed her arm.

"We have to go. Now."

"What's wrong?"

"Ranger is alerting us to danger. Someone's coming."

"Could it be an animal? There are bears and—"

Caleb was already shaking his head as he propelled her toward the front door and pulled his weapon. "Not when he's in work mode. An animal out in the swamp, even a predator, wouldn't pose a threat to us right now. Stay behind me and away from the windows."

Olivia did as he said but glanced out the back French doors. The dock led to a platform where she knew without looking a small, wooden flat-bottom boat would be tied for her trips into the swamp.

Caleb eased the curtains on the front window aside and peered out, just as a barrage of gunfire erupted and tore through the entire front of the cabin.

"Down!" Caleb tackled Olivia to the floor as Ranger dropped at Caleb's command.

Automatic gunfire shattered windows, shredded the curtains and tore chunks from the wood door. Glass flew, nicking his face and arms. They had to get out of there. Now. He rolled off Olivia and grabbed her wrist. Then, with Ranger following beside them, they belly crawled toward the breakfast bar in hopes of putting another barrier between them and their attackers. "Are you okay?"

Olivia looked down at herself, seemingly dazed.

"Olivia! Answer me!" He needed her alert and functioning.

"Yeah. Yeah." Keeping her head low, she brushed glass out of her hair. "I'm okay. But we have to get out of here."

He was already working on that plan as he dialed Zac's number and gave him a very brief update. Since he had agents stationed nearby, it wouldn't take long for help to arrive, but he'd have to stall the gunmen in the meantime. "Well, we definitely can't go out the front."

"Then let's get out the back before they have time to surround the cabin."

"And go where? Into the swamp?"

"There's a boat docked out back. If we can get to it, we can disappear into the swamp without them realizing we're gone."

He ran through his options. Jameson Investigations agents would only take about ten minutes to arrive. They'd considered having a team accompany him and Olivia to the cabin but had decided against it so as not to draw undue attention. The hope had been that just the two of them slipping in near dark might go unnoticed. Plus, the narrow dirt path leading in and the small clearing out front wouldn't leave room to maneuver more than one vehicle if they needed to make a quick escape. Although, the SUV he'd parked facing the road wouldn't do them a bit of good right now.

"Olivia!" A man's voice came from outside the front of the cabin. "You have exactly two minutes to turn over the key you stole from us. You know what's at stake here. If you hand over our property, we'll let you walk away."

Two minutes. It wasn't enough time. Caleb checked out the back door. No sign of anyone out back or in the swamp. "Do you know what they want?"

She shook her head, her brow furrowed in concentration.

"Tick tock, Olivia. Time's a-wastin'," the voice taunted. "No one cares what you try to accuse Tristan of, as long as you don't have evidence to back it up. So, what say you just turn over the flash drive and we'll call it a day?"

Tristan? Olivia's brother? Was he behind this mess?

Olivia glanced toward the back door.

"This is your last chance, Olivia. You were seen going back into the office, and we pulled the video surveillance footage. We know it was you. All you have to do is hand

over that drive. You have one minute left before we launch
a grenade in there and end this once and for all."

So why hadn't they done so already? Was he bluffing?
But why? The only reason Caleb could see was that they
didn't know if she had the flash drive with her. If they blew
the cabin up, whatever evidence they were trying to hide
might still exist out there somewhere. They needed that
flash drive, which was thankfully safe in Angela's hands at
the safe house, before they could eliminate Olivia. Which
might buy them at least a few minutes, but not long enough
for the cavalry to arrive.

He needed to get Olivia and Ranger to safety. Without
her memories, she couldn't tell him if she knew the man is-
suing the orders or if she believed he actually would toss a
grenade to blow up the cabin with them inside. So far, he'd
seen nothing to indicate the man wouldn't make good on
his threat. "We have to get into the swamp and hide until
Zac's agents arrive."

She nodded and shifted her weight, crouching to make
a run for it.

"Ranger. Heel."

Keeping low, Ranger crept to Caleb's side.

He turned to Olivia and studied her as he gauged her
condition. "When I open the door, you stay right with
Ranger, keep low and move as quietly as possible. How
sure are you about the boat being there?"

She lifted her hands to the sides, then let them fall.
"About as sure as I am about anything right now. I think it's
there, just like I thought the key was in the planter, but…"

Her voice trailed off. There wasn't much more she could
say, and staying put wasn't an option.

"Okay, if there's nothing there, we can't stay on the

dock. You'll have to slip off the edge into the water. Just watch out for gators." Certainly not ideal but probably better than the alternative, standing in plain sight with a target on their backs.

"What about you?"

"I'll cover you, and I'll be right behind you."

She squeezed her eyes closed, took a deep breath, then met his gaze and nodded.

"You're running out of time, Olivia," the guy yelled, "and I'm running out of patience."

Caleb ignored the threat. "Ready?"

"Yeah."

He prayed the back door wouldn't squeak as he eased it open enough to squeeze through, then readied himself to return fire as he gestured Olivia and Ranger out behind him. Together, they moved quickly, carefully, toward the end of the dock. He kept his attention focused on their surroundings, trusting Olivia and Ranger to do their part.

Maybe that was surprising. Sure, he knew Ranger, trusted him completely, had worked with him since he first started training. But he was surprised at how easily he trusted Olivia when it came to working together, as if they'd been partnered for years. He wondered if she really was telling the truth about her memory, especially since she knew right where to find the key to the cabin and seemed willing to risk their lives on the fact that a boat was docked out back. But her reaction to her father's photo had seemed genuine. Plus, he'd spoken to the doc about it, and Doc Rogers seemed pretty certain she was telling the truth about the amnesia.

And despite his doubts, he found he trusted her now.

At a soft thud behind him, he turned to find the dock

empty. A moment of terror was followed by instant relief when Olivia popped her head up a second later and grinned as she untied the lines.

He reached the end of the dock and slid off into the boat, if you could call it that. It was more like a punt, flat bottomed with no motor. Not exactly what he'd envisioned, but it was what he had.

She lifted a long pole, then waited. While he'd have preferred to propel the "boat" than make her do it with her injured arm, he didn't dare release his grip on the weapon. He would have to trust she could do this.

The river would take them in either of two directions. One would lead them more toward the clearing out front. The other led deeper into the swamp but would provide cover behind the massive cypress roots almost immediately, as long as they stayed low.

He gestured toward the swamp, and she pushed off instantly. Clearly it was the decision she'd already made, though she'd given him the courtesy of waiting for him to agree with her. The thought brought a smile.

She lifted a brow at him but remained silent.

He scanned her yard as they drifted away, waiting for the building to explode. Not that he wanted her to lose everything, but better the cabin than her life. Maybe they'd just launch the grenade and be done with it.

When she struggled to reposition the pole while crouched in the bottom of the dinghy, he resisted the urge to reach out and take it from her. A few minutes more, and they'd be swallowed up by the forest.

He held his breath.

Ranger panted beside him, crouched low but ready to defend either of them should the need arise.

A gunman rounded the corner of the cabin, pointed toward them and yelled.

Caleb took aim. They weren't out of range yet, but he'd never take the first shot. If they could disappear without a confrontation, he'd opt for that every time.

A second gunman appeared. He turned and yelled something Caleb couldn't hear to a man striding up behind him, then let his weapon hang from the strap around his neck and fished something out of his pocket. He pulled a pin, then lobbed a grenade straight at them.

"Dive!" He hesitated only a fraction of a second, long enough to be sure Ranger obeyed the command, then hit Olivia mid-body, tumbling her over the side with him. He yanked both her and Ranger beneath the murky water.

Pain tore through his side where the boar had hit him. Holding his breath, praying Olivia had had time to do so as well, he struggled to get behind the boat with her in tow. It would help if he could see anything through the cloudy, algae-covered water. Ranger dog-paddled next to him, still in work mode despite the dire circumstances. Ranger, the partner he'd trust above all others, the one who'd saved him after the mess with Rachel.

When he finally broke the surface, a cloudy, brownish swirl surrounded him on the water. He must have opened the wound Doc Rogers had stitched up. Great. If he didn't get eaten by an alligator, he'd have to suffer the good doctor's lecture. Either way, they had to get out of the water. Thankfully, he'd managed to hold onto his weapon. "Swim to the far bank. Ranger, swim."

Olivia ducked beneath the water and swam alongside Ranger, and a moment of panic assailed him. Not for himself, but for Olivia swimming underwater in the dark with a head wound that could begin to bleed through the bandages at any moment. But her strokes were hard and sure.

Ignoring his unease, he rolled onto his back and followed, keeping an eye on the gunmen running toward the shore. The boat was still intact, though capsized between him and them, so it hadn't been a grenade after all, just a flash-bang. But why? There was no way they weren't trying to kill Olivia after all the shots they'd taken. Though other than a graze, none of them so far had found its mark. So, maybe they weren't trying to kill her, but that still didn't feel accurate—or they wanted to disorient her with the flash-bang so they could shoot her. That way, they'd have an opportunity to search her and see if she was carrying the flash drive they wanted. Somehow, he had a feeling the latter was the case.

"Psst."

He risked a quick glance at Olivia, who pointed toward something moving in the water beside him. *Please, don't let it be a gator.*

His prayer was answered. It wasn't an alligator. Instead, a four-foot-long water moccasin swam toward him, its head lifted as if searching for the cause of the commotion, or maybe the source of the blood slowly filling the water.

Seriously? This was the last thing he needed, though whatever bacteria might be flooding his wound from the swamp water could be just as dangerous. But that was a problem for later. He held his breath, cautiously propelling himself backward while trying to keep one eye on the thick snake and the other on the three men standing on the shore watching them.

What were they waiting for? Why didn't they simply open fire and end this?

At least, the snake didn't seem too interested in him.

Then, another man jogged toward them. When he reached the bank, one of the others spoke to him, gesturing toward Olivia and Caleb swimming for the opposite shore. The newcomer stepped forward. "Olivia!"

She went perfectly still.

"Olivia, it's me, Lloyd."

Her fiancé?

He beckoned in their general direction. "Olivia, come on back here and talk to me. Tell me what you've gotten yourself into, and we'll straighten it out."

Without realizing he'd gotten so close to shore, Caleb bumped along the slimy bottom.

"Please, don't stop," Olivia whispered as she scooped her arms beneath his armpits and helped haul him out of the water. "I don't trust him."

He was thankful for that, because he had no intention of stopping to chat. "That makes two of us."

Side by side, with Ranger at his heel, Caleb and Olivia continued to back away.

Caleb kept his weapon trained on Lloyd, since he seemed to be the one in charge. If the man was going to make a move, it would be soon. If he didn't shoot in the next few seconds, they'd be able to disappear into the forest.

The feel of Ranger's flank against his side brought comfort as visions of past failures haunted him. He refused to acknowledge them. He would not fail this time. He would not fail Olivia.

But he couldn't help but wonder what kind of woman would agree to marry a man like the one staring him down from shore. Seemed Olivia had more buried secrets than he might have realized. Was she playing him, after all? Appealing to his sense of honor and duty to...to do what? With no memory of her past, how could she make a conscious decision to do anything?

Of course, she'd conveniently remembered the boat docked out back when there was no other way to escape. But why would she have remembered the monkey trivia? It hadn't benefited them in any way. Had it just been a ploy to excuse any memories she might come up with down the line? That would have to be awfully premeditated. Olivia didn't strike him as that devious.

Then again, he'd trusted Rachel. He'd trusted Todd. What did that say about his character assessment skills?

He shook off the thoughts. There was no time for it now. The moment of truth had come.

Maintaining eye contact, Caleb took another step back, and Lloyd signaled his men.

"Down! Roll!" Caleb dropped, along with Olivia, as Ranger followed his commands. For Olivia's sake, he added, "Roll into the brush."

She was already moving.

As one, the gunmen opened fire. Since his handgun was no match for several men with automatic weapons, he could do nothing but duck, cover and pray Zac's team made it in time.

SEVEN

Olivia knelt in the damp swamp moss, curled into a tight ball behind the trunk of a giant oak tree as shots rang out through the forest, tearing through brush and ricocheting off trees. The last of the setting sun dipped below the horizon. Darkness embraced the swamp, which meant the men were shooting blindly into the forest with no regard for collateral damage.

Caleb bent over her, and Ranger snuggled tight against her side, enveloping her in a cocoon of safety. Did she deserve their protection? Was her life worth the risk they were both taking?

What kind of woman was she that she'd agreed to marry that monster?

Her thoughts turned to Caleb, to all he'd done for her, a total stranger, over the past couple of days. He'd shown nothing but honor, courage and determination to see her safe. Even when her fiancé threatened them and opened fire along with his band of thugs, Caleb still placed himself between her and danger.

"Freeze!" The order came from somewhere across the lake.

Olivia risked lifting her head to peer around the tree.

The cabin's outside floodlights turned on, revealing two men rounding the sides of the house, one from each direction, carrying very large guns. They stopped and stood their ground, using the sides of the cabin for cover, but didn't fire. One of Zac's agents—his voice familiar, though she couldn't place him—called out, "Drop your weapons. Now!"

Lloyd gestured to his men, and they all scattered like rats from a sinking ship.

"Great." Caleb eased back, then held out a hand to help her up without ever taking his eyes from Lloyd. He tracked the other man as he plunged into the lake and swam hard for the opposite shore not far from where they'd taken cover.

Olivia watched him swim, his strokes bold and confident. She tried to swallow but couldn't past the lump of fear clogging her throat. Was he coming for her? Or was he simply trying to escape Zac's men? She pressed her back flat against the tree and willed herself invisible.

"Are you okay?" Caleb whispered, still watching Lloyd.

"Uh-huh." She barely breathed.

When Lloyd reached the opposite shore, he stood and looked over his shoulder. Now, four Jameson Investigations agents stood on the bank, illuminated by the floodlights, guns held ready. Then he scanned the area before disappearing deeper into the brush.

The breath she'd been holding shot from her lungs as she slumped against the tree.

Caleb gripped her hand. "It's okay. He's moving away from us."

"Will Zac's agents shoot him?" Did she want them to? No. Not because of any feelings she still harbored for him—she found it impossible to believe she'd ever loved him in the first place—but because she wouldn't want to see anyone gunned down. She sure would like to see him arrested and put behind bars, though. She squeezed Caleb's ice-cold hand.

"No. They would return fire if they had to, but they won't shoot anyone who doesn't pose an immediate threat." Apparently deciding the gunmen had fled, Caleb released her hand and stepped forward. He pulled his cell phone from his pocket, turned on the flashlight, then used it to signal Zac's men.

"Hey, Caleb," Mason called from where he stood, using a heavy-duty flashlight to scan the lake. "Stay put. We'll get the boat righted and come for you."

"Come get Olivia, then wait here for me. I'm going to see if I can track Lloyd." With that, he turned to Olivia. "Do you remember anything about Lloyd? Do you know what he was talking about?"

"No. Nothing. I'm sorry." Her teeth chattered as shivers tore through her. The ordeal had left her soaking wet with no sun to warm her. The thought of slipping into Caleb's arms for a moment, both for warmth and reassurance briefly flitted through her mind. She dismissed it just as quickly. "But I can tell you one thing."

"Oh?" He lifted a brow. "What's that?"

"The engagement is definitely off."

"Glad to hear it." He laughed, then winced and pressed a hand against his side. It came away bloody.

Her heart skipped a beat, then ratcheted into overdrive. "You're hurt? What happened?"

"It's all right. I just pulled some of the stitches. I'll be fine once Doc sews me back up again."

"You're not really going to try to follow him, are you? There's some light here from the floodlights on the cabin, but a few feet into the swamp beneath the trees, it's pitch-black."

"Thankfully, my cell phone is in a waterproof case, so the flashlight works just fine. And Ranger doesn't need light to track." He reached toward her, noticed the blood on his hand and shot her a sheepish grin. "I need you to wait right here. Mason, Chase and Zac will come for you in a minute. One of them will take you back to the safe house to get cleaned up."

"What about you?"

"The others will come after me. Hopefully, we can find Lloyd before he can make arrangements to be picked up. Then, at least, we might get some answers." He didn't have to add *before someone gets killed*; she was well aware of the ramifications.

A tidal wave of emotions swamped her. At the crest was guilt that others were in danger because of something she'd apparently done, and she couldn't even remember if it was worth the risk. "I don't want to leave you alone in the swamp."

"I won't be alone." His gaze lingered for a moment longer than necessary, then he walked away with Ranger trotting beside him. When they reached the spot where Lloyd had emerged from the swamp, Caleb pulled his weapon and issued the order, "Ranger, track," before they disappeared into the forest.

Olivia waited all of two seconds before pushing away from the tree and going after him. This was her mess. No way would she stand there and do nothing while someone else cleaned up after her.

The spongy ground sucked at her Keds, making her trek through the swamp less than stealthy. Caleb moved fast, but she was able to keep up surprisingly easily, as if traversing the swampland was second nature. Though he moved with nearly predatory silence, she was able to follow subtle signs of his passing—flattened grass, shrubbery left swaying in the humid stillness, the absence of sound from the wildlife who would have stilled at his presence.

How many times had she hiked this land? She couldn't even guess, but she had no doubt this wasn't the first time. The ground was too comfortable, too familiar in a vague sort of way, as if her body and mind reacted instinctively to the peaceful surroundings. She thought of the half-finished paintings in her art studio, the canvases hanging on her bedroom walls. It seemed she chose to surround herself with nature in all aspects of her life. So, what in the world was she doing working as an investment analyst in a city in California?

An image came unbidden—a bedroom, white, sterile, with no sign of the nature paintings that spoke to her heart. Hers? A bed stood in the center, the head elevated, railings on the sides. A pair of clasped hands were superimposed over the vision, one wrinkled, tan, old, the other her own. She lowered her forehead atop the joined hands and cried quietly.

A ringtone some distance ahead of her pulled her from what could only be a memory, if the tears tracking down her cheeks were any indication, and had her pausing. She wiped the tears with the sleeves of her sweatshirt, then stilled and opened her senses, listening for the sound of voices. Was it Caleb's phone? Or was she closing in on Lloyd? And what would she do if she found him? He was supposed to be her fiancé. Which meant he probably had all of the answers she so desperately sought. But would he provide them, or would he simply kill her and be done with it?

When the sounds of the swamp returned to normal—a distant alligator's bellow, an owl's call much closer, and the high-pitched wails of birds that sounded disturbingly human—she inched forward, more cautiously this time.

She scrambled over the knobby knees of cypress roots protruding above the soil. As she passed the first tree, she was grabbed from behind, a hand clamping over her mouth.

She mashed down on the attacker's instep with her heel—if someone had told her a few hours ago she'd wish to be traipsing through the swamp in her spiked heels, she'd have called them crazy—and his hold loosened. But only for a moment before he yanked her back against him in a tight hold and whispered against her ear, "Olivia, it's me. You've got to stay quiet, okay?"

Recognizing Caleb's voice brought a rush of relief, followed closely by rising anger. What was he trying to do, scare her to death? She opened her mouth to say as much.

"Shh."

Then, she realized what was going on. She closed her eyes for a moment while she reined in her temper, then opened them and nodded.

The instant he released her and stepped back, she whirled and shot him a scathing look.

Without giving her time to express her anger, he shook his head, though a small smile played at the corners of his mouth. He gripped her hand firmly in his and started forward again.

They moved together, his strong hand enveloping hers,

reassuring her as they negotiated the swampy terrain. Under other circumstances, the experience might have been enjoyable. She remained silent, understanding the need for stealth. As soon as he realized she could keep up, he increased his pace, his movements swift but confident.

When a dog, she assumed Ranger, started to bark, he dropped her hand and held out a palm to stop her. He put a finger against his lips and gestured for her to stay put.

She crouched low, then inched forward, keeping Caleb in sight without getting in his way or hindering his progress.

He held his cell phone's flashlight aimed at Lloyd, along with his weapon.

"Olivia!" Lloyd screamed. "Make them call this dog off me and let me go. Now!"

"Not gonna happen, buddy." Caleb approached Lloyd. "The only place you're going right now is jail."

Lloyd was on the ground, and Ranger had a hold of his leg. When he'd attacked, Lloyd must have dropped his weapon, because it was nowhere in sight.

Caleb stood over him, weapon and flashlight trained on his head. "Ranger, release."

Ranger did as instructed, then returned to Caleb's side and remained at alert, hackles raised.

"Turn over and put your hands behind your back, Lloyd. Now!" Caleb ordered.

Lloyd grabbed a tree trunk to steady himself as he stood, keeping his hands in plain sight, then raised them in the air.

Olivia held her breath.

"Olivia," he called.

She barely resisted the urge to slap her hands over her ears.

"I know you're out there. I've heard you whine enough

times about how much you miss this place to know you know your way around."

At least one of them seemed to know her.

"Last chance, Lloyd, or I'll set Ranger on you again. Turn around and put your hands behind your back," Caleb ordered.

The slow smile that spread across Lloyd's face sent an ice-cold chill racing down Olivia's spine. "Is that what you want, Olivia? Even knowing what's at stake?"

What was he talking about? Obviously, he thought she understood. She couldn't take it anymore, couldn't stand not knowing anything about herself, about what she'd done and why. About how she'd ever become involved with this monster. She wanted to scream, to rage, to step out from behind her cover and insist he tell her everything.

Caleb took a step closer to him.

Lloyd stepped back. "You don't want to do that, man."

"Oh, yeah, bro. I really do." Lifting his gun, Caleb took another step forward.

"If you take me in, Amy is a dead woman."

Her sister?

Ignoring Caleb's orders, Lloyd raised his voice, directly addressing Olivia. "Didn't Larry give you the picture before the limo crashed?"

Her heart pounded painfully, rocking her hard enough to bring a wave of nausea.

"My men have your sister, Olivia. And unless I return, unharmed, they have orders to kill her."

Olivia stepped out from behind the brush where Caleb had left her.

Sweat slicked his gun hand as he willed her to keep her

distance. He didn't want to have to shoot Lloyd, but the man had fled into the swamp with an automatic weapon that Caleb couldn't locate now. If Olivia got between him and Lloyd, he might not be able to get a clear shot in time to save her.

She stopped at the periphery of the small circle of illumination from his flashlight, lingered in the shadows, hands held out in front of her. "What are you talking about?"

"Our message."

"What message?"

"A picture of your sister in front of a computer with the date clearly showing on the screen—proof of life."

"Proof of…" She pressed her hands against the sides of her head. "I don't understand."

Lloyd's cocky grin slipped a little. "I'm not playing games here, Olivia. Tristan has ordered her execution if you don't turn over that flash drive."

Olivia jerked back, doubling over as if she'd been punched.

No way could she be faking this. Clearly, she didn't know what he was talking about. Her emotional pain was palpable. Caleb had no idea what Olivia might have done, or even what kind of woman she might be, but his every instinct begged him to believe she was telling the truth about her amnesia. She had no way to know the limo she was riding in would crash in the desert and be found by an investigator that worked out of Florida. She couldn't have planned that if she tried. What had he been thinking? Maybe it was easier for him to doubt her honesty. Maybe it had allowed him to keep her at a distance. He'd have to do some soul-searching later on.

But right now, it was time to end this. "Turn and face the tree, Lloyd. On your knees, hands behind your head and interlock your fingers."

"Didn't you hear what I just said?" Lloyd screamed, spittle spraying.

"I heard you. But there's no way you're walking out of this swamp with a weapon, no matter the circumstances." If Olivia's brother had ordered the hit, was Lloyd just an enforcer? Had he gone after Olivia because he wanted to kill her or because he was trying to save her sister's life? Could it be her fiancé wasn't as evil as he appeared?

As confused as Caleb was, he couldn't imagine what Olivia was going through. Her fiancé had apparently tried to kill her. Her brother was involved in something illegal Olivia had obviously somehow found out about, and her sister was in danger of being murdered. And Olivia had no memory of any of it. He wondered if her amnesia had been caused by emotional rather than physical trauma. "Turn around. I'll frisk you, and once I confiscate any weapons, I'll let you walk out of here."

Olivia gasped, but Caleb had no choice. He could take Lloyd into custody, but he'd have to turn him over to the police. It wasn't likely he'd get a chance to interrogate him or make a deal if he felt it was warranted. And even if the local authorities did allow Zac some kind of access, cutting through all the red tape might take more time than Amy had.

Lloyd seemed to contemplate his offer, then his gaze skipped to Olivia. "I want the flash drive, too. Do you have it on you, or did you hide it in the cabin? I'll walk out of here with no weapons, but I can't return to Tristan without that drive, or he *will* kill Amy. I'm trying to help you here, Olivia. Why aren't you cooperating, honey? I don't understand."

The use of the obviously disingenuous endearment rankled Caleb.

"How are you trying to help me?" Olivia flung an arm out toward the lake. "By launching a grenade into my boat?"

"Aww, now, baby, it wasn't a real grenade. Just, you know, like an attention-getter. I would never have let anyone hurt you."

"And the machine guns your guys were shooting at me?" Her voice took on a hysterical edge.

He lifted his hands and offered a smile reminiscent of a snake oil salesman, shooting for charm and missing the mark by a mile. "You weren't hit, were you?"

Olivia scowled and shook her head. She caught her bottom lip between her teeth, as she often seemed to when confused.

"Now." Obviously inspired by her silence, probably thinking he was gaining ground, Lloyd started to lower his hands and took a step forward.

Caleb firmed his grip on the weapon. "Don't you move."

"Oh, right, yeah." He put his hands back up. "Come on, Olivia, why don't we forget about all this, and you can come home with me? We'll go to Tristan together and give him the flash drive, then we'll collect Amy, and I'll take the two of you out to dinner somewhere nice."

Caleb had let Lloyd talk long enough. "She's not going anywhere with you."

"Oh? And who exactly are you?"

Caleb had no intention of answering the man's questions. Nor would he allow Olivia to answer any, so he snapped, "Turn and face the tree before the rest of my team gets here. If you're not gone before they arrive, you will lose the opportunity."

Olivia's mouth dropped open. "Are you seriously letting him go?"

"Olivia—"

"No. Don't Olivia me. Why would you let him go?"

He'd made a big leap deciding to believe her, to trust her; now she was going to have to do the same and put her trust in him. Keeping his gun steady on Lloyd, who still stood with his hands raised, he sidestepped until he reached Olivia, then pitched his voice low. "I won't set him free with a weapon. Not that he can't get more, but at least I'll know I didn't let him go armed. But if what he's saying is true about your sister, what choice do I have?"

She shook her head, but then she went still. "What if I go with him?"

"No. Absolutely not."

"Maybe I can figure out what's going on. If I go with him, I can talk to Tristan. He's my brother, right? Why would he want to hurt me or...or Amy?"

"Look, Olivia. There's no time to figure this out right now, and you are not running off half-cocked. At least, not on my watch. We have to step back, assess and buy ourselves and Amy some time." But the thought gave him an idea. "Face the tree, Lloyd. My offer expires in three seconds."

Lloyd stared Caleb down a moment longer.

"Two." Movement in the trees alerted Caleb his team was close. It also alerted Lloyd, which was what they'd intended. Otherwise, no one would have heard a sound.

"Are you really going to allow this, Olivia?" he asked. "What is wrong with you, woman?"

Caleb's mind raced. They needed a way to buy time while they sorted out this mess and came up with a plan of action. A way that didn't involve Olivia going anywhere with this man. "She hit her head in the limo crash and has amnesia. The doctor said it's probably temporary, but she has to give herself time to heal. That's why we were at the cabin, to see if we could jog some memories loose. Unfortunately, you and your thugs showed up before we could make any headway. Now, turn around and kneel. I will let you go, and you can give Tristan a message. She needs time to recover her memories. Right now, she doesn't even know anything about this flash drive you're talking about."

It was close enough to the truth, though he could only assume it was the drive they already had in their possession. Even with their experts working to decode it, they would need time.

Lloyd narrowed his gaze at Olivia. "Is that true?"

She nodded.

With a muttered curse, he turned, knelt and interlaced his fingers behind his head.

As promised, Caleb patted him down, then pulled a handgun from a holster against his side and another from the waistband of his pants. He found the automatic weapon a few feet away in the mud. After confiscating all three, he stepped back to Olivia. "Get out of here."

Lloyd stood and turned to face them, the knees of his tan suit pants covered in muck. He kept his hands at his sides. "I don't suppose I could hitch a ride out of here."

Caleb took Olivia's hand in his. "Just be grateful I'm

letting you go at all. And make sure you pass on the message to Tristan. Olivia needs time."

"How will I contact you?"

Caleb rattled off the number for one of the burner phones Angela kept on hand and waited while Lloyd programmed it into his own phone. "Why don't you give me a number to reach you at?"

Lloyd grinned. "Let's just say, don't call us, we'll call you."

"Fine. Ranger, heel." As soon as the dog returned to Caleb's side, Lloyd took off through the woods. Caleb turned and led Olivia back in the direction they'd come from, confident his back was covered as Zac's team fell in behind them and provided cover.

Olivia squeezed his hand. "Do you think that was the right move? Telling him I have amnesia?"

He honestly had no idea. He was running on empty. He was already exhausted when he found her wandering the desert. Now, he was beyond exhausted, injured and bleeding fairly heavily. He couldn't help but question why God had chosen him to find Olivia. Surely, there had to be someone less of a mess He could have selected. "It was the only thing I could think of on the spur of the moment that would buy us time to decode the flash drive and decipher what we're handing over to him."

"What if we just give him the flash drive and get Amy back? What difference does it make?" She yanked her hand out of his and wrapped both arms around herself. "It's not like I even know what's on it, and you know what? I'm starting to hope I never remember."

"Hey." When he realized she was shivering, he wrapped his arm around her shoulders and pulled her close.

She stiffened for a moment, then leaned into his embrace. They kept walking that way, and she easily kept pace, as if she were meant to be exactly where she was—at his side.

He clamped down on the thoughts. First of all, the woman was engaged. Even if she had insisted the engagement was off, once she regained her memories, she could well go right back to her old life, including her fiancé. Though, Caleb hoped she had better judgment than that. And second, he had no intention of opening his heart to anyone after his wife and his best friend had both deceived him. Even if he wanted to, he couldn't take the risk after their betrayal cut him so deeply and sent him spiraling into a well of despair he still hadn't fully pulled himself out of.

And he'd already gotten dangerously close to caring about Olivia Delaney's well-being.

He slid his arm from her shoulders and slowed for Mason to catch up to them. Then, he fell into step beside Mason, keeping his gaze firmly averted from Olivia. He didn't want to know how she might or might not have reacted to his stepping away. It was for the best, and he'd do well to remember that. "How much of that did you hear?"

Mason glanced back over his shoulder as he walked. "Enough to know you probably bought us some time."

"But was it the right thing to let him go?" Even though it was the only path he could see at the time, he still beat himself up over setting a criminal free.

Mason shrugged, understanding the lesser of two evils. "Who knows? It was the decision that felt right in your gut at the time, so now we move forward with what we've got. Second-guessing solves nothing."

As Caleb well knew, when he wasn't busy feeling sorry

for himself. His eyes involuntarily flitted to Olivia, his thoughts to all she'd endured, to the strength she'd summoned to hold up beneath the weight of it all. Even now, trampling through the swamp by flashlight, damp and covered in muck, she was incredibly beautiful, both inside and out. Hopefully, she'd stay that way once she remembered who she was.

I'm starting to hope I never remember. Guilt swamped him when he realized he hadn't responded when she said that. With a sigh, he caught up to her. "Olivia. Hey."

She slowed to meet his stride and kept walking. "I'm sorry. I had to step away for a moment, but we never finished talking. I can't even begin to imagine how difficult this situation must be for you. If after all of this you just want to turn that flash drive over to Tristan and go back to your life, I'll help you. But somehow, I have a feeling you wouldn't have taken anything if you didn't think it was important. I believe in you, and I can't believe the person you are right now isn't the same person you were before your memories faded. I won't believe that."

A hint of a smile played at the corner of her mouth. "Thank you, Caleb. Not just for believing in me, but for everything you've done to help me."

Ranger bumped her hip with his head, and she reached down to pet him. "You, too, Ranger."

Caleb couldn't help but grin. He might not be able to offer Olivia anything more than this moment, but for now, he would help her see this through.

"So?" she asked. "Where does this leave us? Where do we go from here?"

"Well, I don't know about you, but right now all I want

to do is get cleaned up." Have Doc restitch his side. "And sit down to a hot meal and a few minutes of peace."

"And then?"

"And then we figure out what's on that flash drive, take down your evil brother and fiancé and save your sister. Sound like a plan?"

"Yes, it does." Her soft laughter drifted through the swamp like a beacon of hope amid utter chaos.

EIGHT

Now that she knew her pseudonym from the artwork in the cabin, Olivia was ready to get to work learning more about herself. She settled with a mug of tea in front of the computer Angela showed her to in the living room. "Thank you, Angela. For everything."

"Of course. Just give a yell if you need anything else." She leaned over Olivia and rested a hand on the back of her chair. "And just in case you were wondering, Dr. Rogers finished suturing and admonishing Caleb and sent him to get cleaned up." With a wink, she walked away.

What did it matter to Olivia where Caleb was? Just because she glanced at the doorway every few minutes didn't mean she was searching for him. Although she'd known when he left the makeshift exam room with the doctor because Ranger got up from her side and padded out of the room, probably to go meet him. And even if she was curious, maybe she just wanted to see if he was okay after being injured protecting her—again. It wasn't like she was interested in him as anything more than a friend. Even if her engagement had already ended in her mind.

Her gaze shifted to her left hand, where no ring adorned her finger. Try as she might, she couldn't envision one ever

having been there. Could she have broken off the engagement before she lost her memory? It didn't seem likely that
she would have lost the ring in the accident, and she didn't
have a tan line indicating she usually wore one.

And what did she think of her fiancé? She didn't believe he had her best interest at heart, not for an instant.
He was handsome, in a snooty, arrogant sort of way, but
he was too slick, too deceptive, not the kind of man she'd
go for. Not like Caleb.

"Ugh." She chased the thought away. Caleb had been
kind, had protected her when she feared for her life. It was
only natural she would see him as her hero and look up
to him. There was nothing wrong with that, but it didn't
mean anything more. Especially not when she was such a
mess. Besides, even if there had been anything budding between them, Caleb had held her at arm's length ever since
finding out she was engaged, and she couldn't blame him.
Even that was noble of him.

She swiped her hands over her face, smoothed her hair
into a ponytail and tied it with a scrunchie from her wrist.
She'd never accomplish anything if she sat there brooding
all day. And she would need more than the few hours sleep
she'd managed at some point, too. She glanced at the clock
in the corner of the computer's screen—already 10:00 a.m.
Not surprising after the ordeal in the swamp, then getting
debriefed and cleaned up. But she should still have a few
more hours in her to start searching social media for any
mention of her pen name.

She cleared her mind of everything, mostly Caleb, since
there wasn't much else rattling around in there besides
questions she couldn't answer. Then she froze, her fingers hovering over the keyboard. Was that why everything

about Caleb seemed so appealing? Aside from his rugged good looks, he was someone kind to hold onto when she had no one else. The thought rankled, and she prayed she wasn't that shallow or needy or selfish.

"Okay," she muttered. "Enough procrastinating. There might not be much information available on Olivia Delaney, but let's see how Olivia Malcolm spends her time."

She started with a Google search, which brought pages and pages of results. "Well, well, well. What do we have here?"

She started with Facebook and immediately clicked on her friends. When she searched Lloyd Wellington, she received a no results message. Of course, some people just used their first name, so she typed in Lloyd. Still no results. Giving up for now, she typed in Tristan's name, only to receive the same message. Hmm. The Facebook account was under her pseudonym, so maybe she only friended work relations there. With that in mind, she tried Amy's name. Optimistic that she was finally getting somewhere, she clicked on the suggestion that popped up.

She was rewarded with Amy's profile. There wasn't much posted, and what was tended to be reposts of information from the Delaney Investments page, mostly advertisements. There was a picture, though, of Amy smiling and waving at someone.

Olivia enlarged the image, then squinted and leaned forward to study the background—an office building with palm trees lining the courtyard. Familiar? Maybe. It might be the one Angela had shown her, but from a different angle.

Giving up that avenue of pursuit, she switched to her own profile and clicked on the photos. She'd posted pictures of her artwork, pictures that appeared to have been taken in the swamp, pictures of wildlife that seemed native to Florida, including the monkeys. There didn't appear to be any photos of her or friends.

Her last posted image had been a little more than a year ago. So, what had happened? She didn't have to scroll long before she came to a post saying she'd been called to California because her father had passed away and that she'd be back soon. Butterflies flittered in her stomach. Beneath the post was a video. She clicked on the link and listened to "Amazing Grace," the hymn obviously important to her. The opening lines, *Amazing grace! How sweet the sound. That saved a wretch like me! I once was lost, but now am found, was blind, but now I see*, moved something deep inside of her.

Her memories didn't return, but a sense of peace flowed through her, and she understood the message that God cares for you during your darkest hours, that forgiveness and mercy are possible. Why had that message been so important to her that she'd have posted it along with the news about her father? Was he the one who'd needed redemption, or did she? The answer was there, just on the periphery of awareness. If she could just reach out and grab hold. The hymn meant something to her.

"Hey." Caleb interrupted her musings, and whatever memories might have been dancing along the edge of awareness skittered away. He pulled a chair from one of the other desks set up next to hers and dropped onto it.

Ranger dropped a bone, then barked once as if in greeting and lay down at their feet.

The fact that she'd missed them both came as no surprise. The intensity of the emotions did.

"So…" Caleb gestured toward the screen. "Find anything useful?"

"I did, actually." She showed him the post. Better to deal with business than examine her feelings too closely. "At least, I think it's useful. For just a moment, I thought I was going to remember something, but then I lost it."

He leaned forward and folded his arms on the desk. "So keep going. Let's see what we can find."

She did as he suggested, scrolling through several other social media accounts and finding more of the same. It seemed most of her posts regarded artwork and most of her contacts lived in the same world. The groups she belonged to all had something to do with art or nature. So, hobby accounts. And like with her Facebook account, her last posts had been dated about one year earlier.

She also found a dedicated website for her artwork, a blog about her jaunts into the swamp, and an Etsy shop, none of which had been updated anytime recently.

From everything she could find, she hadn't returned to her life in Florida after her father had passed, and Olivia Malcolm had ceased to exist. And yet, the cabin hadn't seemed abandoned. Everything had smelled clean and fresh. When she'd picked up the photo of her and her father, it hadn't been covered in dust. "A cleaning person."

"Huh?" Caleb narrowed his gaze at the screen. "Where?"

She minimized the window and swiveled her chair to face him. "From looking at my social media, it seems I've been gone from Florida for the past year, so how was my cabin so clean? The belongings all seemed to be mine, so I didn't rent it out. Unless I returned at some point, someone had to have cleaned it recently. Is there a way to find out if I took a flight back from California in the past year?"

He shifted his chair back and stood so suddenly Ranger scrambled to his feet. "Sorry about that, boy. Come on. I don't see why Angela can't track that information down."

For the first time since waking alone and afraid in the desert, a sense of optimism surged through her. Her memories were still there; she knew it. And sooner or later, she'd be able to access them, and they might finally get some answers. For now, she could find out if she returned to Florida at any point. And if she hadn't, whatever cleaning company she'd hired might know how long she'd planned to be gone. At last, they were finally making forward progress instead of simply running from the past and hiding.

They found Angela at her work station in the kitchen.

Caleb pulled out a stool on one side of her and gestured for Olivia to sit, then took the stool on the other side of her so they'd both be able to watch the screen should Angela uncover anything helpful. "Can you tell if Olivia boarded any flights over the past year?"

Angela minimized the screen displaying what appeared to be a list of financial data. "Sure. What's up?"

He explained their theory, and she began to search for cleaners in the area, pulling up website after website, then dismissing each in turn. "Oh, and also, I gave one of the burner phone numbers to Lloyd Wellington so he could contact us."

She nodded, clearly distracted. "Mason told me, and it's already being monitored."

"Thanks."

"You bet."

It amazed Olivia how well Zac's team worked together, more like family than anything else, and she couldn't help but wonder if she'd found that same sense of camaraderie with her coworkers at Delaney Investments. Surely she had some friends there.

Angela pulled up another website then paused. "Olivia, do you know the password for your bank account?"

She opened her mouth, as if the password would automatically be there to retrieve. Nothing. She shook her head.

"That's okay. I figured if we could get into your bank account, we could see if you'd paid for an airline flight or a cleaning company. But there are other ways we can figure it out." Angela searched for cleaning companies, printed out a list of those within the immediate vicinity of the cabin, then split the list and handed them each a batch to contact. "Get to it, guys."

Olivia retreated to the far corner of the room and pulled a chair out from the table to sit where she could keep an eye on the other two just in case they got a hit.

She dialed the first number, went through the spiel they'd concocted, that she'd hired a cleaning company before and wanted to use the same one again but couldn't remember which one it had been. Would she be forgiven for the white lie in order to get answers? She prayed God would understand. If there was any other way, she'd have chosen the more honest path.

By her third call, she was about ready to give up. Maybe she'd simply hired a local, not a company, who came once a week and was on an automatic payment schedule or something.

Caleb lurched away from where he leaned against the wall, then gestured a scribbling motion to Angela, who immediately jumped up and handed him a pad and pen.

Olivia thanked her current call and hung up.

A moment later, Caleb did the same. "Okay, I found it.

You hired a cleaning company via online form the same day as, and only a few hours after, the limo crash. You paid by credit card using their website."

Angela checked the name he jotted down, then began an intensive search. Although, what she was looking for, Olivia had no idea.

Olivia frowned, racking her brain. Was she somehow forgetting things that happened after the crash, too? That didn't make sense. How could she have hired anyone when she hadn't had internet access until they reached the safe house.

"Not only did you provide a generous tip, you paid extra for a rush job, said you needed it done as quickly as possible." Caleb lowered himself onto his stool, wincing as he did so. When she started toward him, he held up a hand as if he were okay.

She let him be. "So, what does all of that mean?"

"Well…" He smoothed a hand over his buzz cut that seemed to have grown in a bit over the past couple of days. "When I explained I was an investigator working a case involving the cabin, he got nervous, said the place was trashed when the crew went in."

Olivia dropped onto her stool. Trashed? Only hours after the limo crash? *Before* she'd even considered returning to Florida? "I don't understand."

"I do." Angela held up a finger, typed for a couple of seconds, then shot something off to the printer. "I was looking for a connection between the cleaning company and Delaney Investments, and I didn't find anything. The company seems clean. But when I returned to searching for a flight Olivia might have taken, I discovered she booked a flight to Florida for the day before the crash."

Olivia searched for the memory, frustrated by her lack of knowledge. "I don't remember any of this. Did I fly here and return to California the same day?"

"Well, despite the amnesia, this time your memory isn't failing you. You never boarded the flight."

"I didn't?"

Angela shook her head.

"Maybe, instead of being here, I should go to my house in California and search for my memories there."

Angela made eye contact, her expression filled with sympathy. "I'm so sorry, Olivia, but your house in California burned down late last night. Nothing was salvageable."

Olivia paused, waiting for the pain and sense of loss to hit her. But it never came. She was sad, sure. There were probably personal items with sentimental value she couldn't determine right now, but it was as if Angela were talking about a stranger's home. So, where did that leave them?

"Angela!" A guy who looked to be about fifteen rushed into the room. His short, dark hair stuck straight up in tufts as he waved a stack of pages the size of an encyclopedia. He shoved a pair of thick, black-framed glasses with duct tape around one arm back up his nose. "I did it."

Angela shot him a thousand-watt smile. "I knew you would, Einstein."

The boy stopped when he noticed Olivia sitting next to her.

"It's okay." Caleb stood and took the pages from the guy and handed them over to Angela. "Einstein, this is Olivia Delaney. Olivia, this is Emeril Eastman, better known as Einstein. A genius we were fortunate enough to scoop up straight out of college, though Zac still laments the fact that we have to share him with the FBI."

Olivia stood and offered her hand.

Einstein grinned and stuck out a hand to pump hers. "Pleased to meetcha."

"It's nice to meet you, too. Thank you for helping me."

"Sure thing. Is it okay if I…" He rolled his hand and looked to Angela.

"Yes, you can talk in front of her."

"Great!" He rubbed his hands together, clearly thrilled with his work and eager to share his accomplishments. "I was able to crack the code used on the flash drive. And let me tell you, it's not just files. This thing is an encryption key."

Everything in Olivia went still.

He slapped a hand on the stack of papers, and she caught a glimpse of the decoded financial information. "And boy is this code a doozy. Whoever wrote it didn't just copy files from the company, they locked down the whole system. No one at Delaney Investments can access their files or their financials."

Me. I wrote that code.

"No wonder those guys want this drive back," Einstein said. "They need to physically put this drive back into one of their computers to decrypt everything."

"Is that all that's on the flash drive?" Angela asked.

"Nope. Once I was able to get through the code, it was easy enough to decipher what was being hidden. It's a ton of evidence of corruption."

The money laundering scheme. The drug cartel. Her father's death under suspicious circumstances. Her sister's kidnapping. Tristan. Lloyd. The encryption key.

All of it plowed through her with the force of a batter-
ing ram. She staggered beneath the weight of memories
she couldn't hope to sort through as quickly as they pum-
meled her. Pain tore through her skull.

"Hey." Caleb frowned. "You okay?"

No. I'm far from okay. She flattened her hands against
the sides of her head and squeezed—hard. "I'm fine."

Caleb's arm came around her. "Get the doc back here."

"No. I'm fine. I… It's just a headache. I just need to lie
down in a dark room for a little while." Tears leaked from
the corners of her eyes. Not only from the pain coursing
through her, but from the fact that they were all in a lot
more danger than any of them realized.

Caleb grabbed a couple of sausage, egg and cheese bis-
cuits and two boxes of hash browns from the pile on the
table and set them on a tray along with a variety of sauce
packets. Then he added an oversize mug of coffee for himself and the tea Olivia seemed to prefer and headed to her
room. He stood outside her door for a moment, hesitant to
wake her if she'd been able to sleep. He wasn't sure what
happened to her the day before, but something had. A result of the accident?

Doc Rogers said the results of all her tests came back
normal. Could he have missed something? He'd taken care
of Zac's agents since the inception of Jameson Investigations, and he took his job seriously, but anyone could miss
something. Right? No one was infallible.

Caleb balanced the tray on one arm and knocked softly.
If she answered, great. If not, he'd let her sleep.

"Come in."

He eased the door open a crack and peered inside. He

needn't have worried. She sat in an armchair, feet propped on an ottoman, staring out the window.

"Can I come in?"

"Sure."

Leaving the door open, he crossed the room and handed her the tray of food. Then he grabbed a small side table, pulled it next to her chair and dragged another chair from the corner. With the table between them, he sat, and she placed their meal down. "I thought you might be hungry."

"Not really, but thank you." She was already dressed, her hair still damp, a few ringlets clinging to her cheeks. She pulled the blanket tighter around herself.

"How did you sleep?" He set about unwrapping the sandwiches. If the food was there and easily accessible, maybe she'd give it a try.

"I didn't actually get too much sleep."

"Still have the headache? I could get you something for it if you want." He rested his hands on the arms of his chair and started to push himself up, careful of his stitches lest Doc Rogers have to sew him up a third time.

"No, please. I'm fine." She snuggled deeper into her own chair and finally pulled her gaze from the rising sun to face him. "I... I never made the flight back to Florida because I needed the information I copied onto the flash drive I gave Angela. The only way to access that information was at a staff meeting that was scheduled for the day before the flight. Unfortunately, that meeting was postponed. I had planned to gather whatever evidence I could, then come back here to sort it all out before going to the authorities. That code, the one that locked up Delaney Investments's files and accounts? I wrote that. Did you know I majored in computer science? I was even president of my college's coding club."Everything in him went still. Had she lied to him all along? Just when he'd started to believe in her?

"My memory returned yesterday."

"Hey, that's great." Relief he didn't dare examine too closely poured through him. It only took a fraction of an instant to realize she wasn't exactly happy with what she'd remembered. He opened his mouth to ask the first question that came to mind—was she really engaged to Lloyd Wellington—then snapped it shut just as quickly. His professional integrity when it came to Olivia was teetering on a tightrope.

"No, Caleb, it's not." Her mouth firmed into a thin line, and she lowered her gaze. "The next day, after the meeting finally took place, when a gunman opened fire on me on a crowded street, I knew I had to go straight to the police station. I never made it." She swallowed. "I'm so very sorry, but I've put you and your team into a way more dangerous situation than I realized, and I will never forgive myself for that."

"Hey..." He reached for her hand, but she tucked it beneath the blanket. "Whatever's going on, we'll figure it out. At least, now, we'll have some idea where to start."

"No." She shook her head, her expression adamant. "*We* won't do anything. I'm going to leave this morning. I thought of just slipping out, but with your guards on duty twenty-four-seven, I figured I'd never make it past the door. And then I realized I couldn't sneak away and risk you coming to look for me. So, I waited to tell you and say goodbye."

Fear crept up his spine. No way could he let her face whatever had her so terrified on her own. He started to ramble, set on getting his point across before she could bail. "Jameson Investigations takes on cases like this all the time. It's what we do—protect people, help them through difficult times, investigate situations when people are in trouble. We are your safest bet for getting out of this alive."

"Don't you get it?" she yelled. Twin crimson patches rose on her cheeks, at last bringing some color to her complexion. She'd been totally pale since the headache hit her the day before.

Except…it wasn't a headache, he realized suddenly. Her memories had returned full force and overwhelmed her. Okay. That he could deal with. Plus, the fact that she'd been telling the truth all along meant that he hadn't lost his edge when he'd believed in her. He thought he'd lost his ability to read people, but maybe he'd only lost faith in his instincts. Rachel didn't break him after all. And maybe his instincts were more spot-on than he thought.

"I was never going to make it out of this alive," she admitted quietly. "I'm sorry I ever got you involved, sorry I dragged any of you into this. Thank you for trying to help me, Caleb, but I've got it from here."

Panic assailed him, and he searched for a way to reason with her. He took a deep breath and strove for a calm, laid-back demeanor. "I'll tell you what. Why don't you just tell me what you remembered, and I'll help you figure out what your next move should be? Then, if you still think you should go it alone, I'll leave you be."

"You don't have a choice, Caleb."

"Everyone has a choice, Olivia," he countered.

She blew up a breath, ruffling the wisps of hair beginning to dry and curl around her face.

Taking that as a weakening in her armor, he pushed forward. "And while we're talking, you can at least eat something before you take off on your own. Who knows when you might get the chance again?"

She massaged the bridge of her nose, then lowered her hand and sighed.

When she sat up and shrugged off the blanket, he thought she might make a run for it. But she perched on the edge of her seat, knee bouncing up and down. "Honestly, I wouldn't even know where to start. That's why I didn't say anything yesterday. Not because I wanted to deceive you or block you out or anything, just because the memories crashed over me all at once so suddenly that I practically crumbled beneath their intensity. I needed time to sort through them before I could talk about any of it."

"I can certainly understand that. And you've had time." He picked up a hash brown, opened a random sauce packet without bothering to look and dipped it. It landed like a lead ball in his stomach, but he wanted to put her at ease. As skittish as she appeared, he knew he was barely keeping her in her chair. He held the sandwich out to her. "Please. Just eat something and talk to me. I haven't let you down yet, have I?"

"No. You haven't." She hesitated but then finally took the sandwich from him.

"Good." He took another bite, allowing her time to hash through whatever she needed to.

She took a small bite, chewed and swallowed before saying another word. Then she set the sandwich down on the table and wiped her fingers on a napkin. "I've lived in Florida since I left home for college. A year ago, I received a call from my father's attorney that my father had a heart attack and I needed to return home immediately."

"The call came from his attorney? Not family?"

She nodded. "My brother and sister are quite a bit older than I am. They're my half siblings, I think Angela mentioned that? Anyway, our relationship has always been a little rocky. My sister and I mostly get along okay, but she was the one to find Dad. She went in the ambulance with him, and when I finally arrived, she was an emotional mess. And my brother, well… Estranged would be a nice way to define the relationship between the two of us, I suppose. Both of my siblings resented their stepmother—my mother—and the strong relationship my father had with us. But Tristan was worse. He was already twelve when I was born, and he was jealous, mean…even vicious. Then as a teen, he got mixed up with drugs. When I found out, I told our father, and Tristan never forgave me."

Caleb set his food aside, unable for force any more down. It probably didn't matter anyway. It seemed, once she got started, she would purge herself of everything.

"He tormented me from then on, but I suppose I'm getting ahead of myself."

Caleb shifted so he could watch her as she spoke. The pain etched so clearly on her face had him wanting to reach out to her, offer some kind of comfort. But he knew too well, some wounds couldn't be healed.

"Tristan was sent to rehab, and he recovered, but even though he got off the drugs, he still owed his dealer money. He took on a role working for my father's company, and my father was thrilled. As Dad aged, Tristan took on more and more responsibility, until he was practically running Delaney Investments while my father semiretired. Amy worked beneath him, and everything seemed to be going well. But it wasn't for me. I always wanted to be an artist. My dad offered me a deal. I'd go to college and get a degree in business so I could return to the company if my art didn't work out, and he'd do everything in his power to help me succeed on my chosen path. Though it saddened my dad, he understood my passions lay elsewhere, and he offered all the support in the world as I tried to make my own name in the art world." Her voice hitched. "He came to Florida often. We spent weeks at a time together, hanging out in the swamp, him fishing while I painted."

She stopped talking and stared off into the distance, no doubt too far in the past for Caleb to reach.

So he waited, biding his time while she ordered her thoughts. He stood and grabbed a box of tissues from the nightstand and set it next to her.

"Thank you." She sniffed, wiped her tears. "After my father passed away, I returned to California. I found a journal in his belongings. Apparently, he'd suspected what was going on, and he found evidence of shell corporations. He had an idea of who was involved. He made notes about it in his journal, but he needed more proof."

"What did he think was happening?"

"Turns out Tristan also went to work for his dealer at the same time he started at Delaney Investments, then worked his way up the ladder until he became a high-ranking member of the drug cartel and started laundering money through our father's business. When Dad found out, he confronted Tristan. He was furious. He threatened to restructure the company with Amy in charge and him out in the street with nothing."

"But he didn't follow through."

She shook her head. "Apparently, while my father was spending much of his time in Florida with me, Tristan had siphoned more and more money and stock for himself, making him the majority stockholder. Before my father could tell anyone what was going on or take steps to correct it, he had a heart attack."

"So you stayed to continue where he left off?"

"Sort of. Honestly, at first I stayed because I felt guilty over not being there for my dad. Then I found the journal. It took me months to finish what my father started. Tristan was careful. He tried to keep me from coming to work there, but Amy pushed for me, said she wanted me to come home."

"Do you think she was part of this?"

"No. Not at all. But my dad…well…he wasn't a trusting man. He and I were close, very close, but Amy and he were not. Amy and Tristan's mom walked out when they were little, and I guess my dad was distant with them. That distance grew. Amy got along with my mom and me okay, but after my mom passed away, she grew even further apart from my dad."

"I'm sorry," he murmured, and she shrugged.

"It was a long time ago. But…he wouldn't have gone to Amy with this, and she probably wouldn't have helped if he had." She inhaled a deep shaky breath. "It was up to me. And I gave up the life I loved to stay in California and try to see to my father's last wishes."

"Olivia…" How could Caleb broach the subject on his mind when she was clearly in so much pain? It might be better to simply have Angela look into it instead, but the idea of leaving Olivia out of the loop sat about as well as the few bites of food he'd managed to choke down. "Was your father in poor health?"

"No." Distracted, she shredded a napkin into small strips, piling them on the tray. "He used to walk miles a day through the swamp and forest with me. He ate a healthy diet, didn't smoke or drink. By all accounts, he was a healthy older man."

Caleb sucked in a deep breath, blew it out slowly. "Do you think the heart attack could have been anything else?"

Her gaze shot to his. "What do you mean?"

Even he wasn't sure quite where he was going with this or why his gut was leading him down such a dark road. "It's just, the way you recounted it, the timing seems odd. He finds out about the laundering, threatens to remove your brother from the company, then has a heart attack."

"What else could it have been?"

"There are ways to kill someone, drugs that can mimic a heart attack."

"Drugs Tristan might have had access to."

"Was there an autopsy?"

She shook her head and shot to her feet, hands fisted at her sides. "No. We didn't have any reason to suspect foul play. At least, I didn't until after I found the journal."

He stood facing her, took both of her hands in his. "Listen to me, Olivia. Please. I know it can't be easy for you, and I completely understand what it's like not to trust anyone. But I'm asking you. Please. Let me help you. Trust me enough to at least try to get to the bottom of this and save Amy."

"I don't want anyone else to get hurt because of me."

"I can't promise that won't happen, and I won't lie to you. All I can tell you is, you're worth the risk."

Her gaze met his. She looked so lost, so frightened. Yet, he saw such strength in her, such determination.

He had no idea how it happened, who might have leaned in first, but the next thing he knew, his lips brushed against hers, once, twice, and then she was in his arms as he kissed her.

"Hey, oh, I…uh. Sorry." Angela held out a cell phone. "The burner phone with the number you gave Lloyd is ringing. The call is from a blocked number, but we'll try to trace it."

Lloyd. Caleb pulled back. What had he done? "I'm so sorry, Olivia."

She shook her head and turned to look out the window.

Whatever trust he might have been on the verge of obtaining had just probably shattered into a million pieces. He took the phone from Angela and answered.

NINE

Olivia stared out the window where black clouds had already begun to build. Unusual so early in the day. She remembered that now—remembered everything about the home she loved so much. She longed to return to her cabin on the outskirts of the swamp, where she could immerse herself in the sights and sounds of nature anytime. She'd stayed away too long.

Caleb had taken a call on the burner phone, presumably from Lloyd, then left the room with Angela to find Zac and work out some kind of plan on what they should do next.

Olivia would want in on that. Eventually. But, for the moment, she was content to stand at the window, watching the storm roil, knowing it would soon rage, so symbolic of her own emotions.

Topping the heap was the fact that she'd kissed Caleb. She didn't feel any guilt as far as betraying Lloyd went. She and Lloyd Wellington had been over months ago. Thankfully, she remembered that now. The fact that she could ever have fallen for a monster like that had had her concerned about what kind of person she might be. But she'd never been in love with Lloyd, only with the illusion he created.

A soft knock had her turning toward the door. "Come in."

The door creaked open, and Angela poked her head inside. "I'm sorry to intrude, but we're having a meeting to go over everything. I thought you might like to know."

She wouldn't examine her disappointment that Caleb wasn't the one to come for her. Not now, anyway. "Sure. Thank you."

The other woman started to back away and ease the door shut, then she studied Olivia more closely and stepped inside instead. "Are you doing okay?"

Was she? Olivia grimaced. She had no idea.

"I'm here if you want to talk." Angela strode across the room and took the seat Caleb had been sitting in.

Olivia missed him, missed having him near. It seemed he lent her strength.

"I'm a good listener." Angela crossed one leg over the other, smoothed her skirt and studied the coming storm as if she had all day to wait for Olivia to open up.

And Olivia realized suddenly that she missed that, having a friend to confide in, to bounce ideas off of, to laugh with. Not that she was in any mood to laugh right now.

"It can't be easy remembering everything all at once like that, especially since your brother and fiancé, two people you should have been able to trust, were involved."

"Former fiancé." Olivia sank back into her chair. Her heart had broken when she found out her and Lloyd's entire relationship was a lie, an effort by her brother to keep track of her movements and let him know if she was getting close to the truth about what was going on at the company. She probably never would have figured it out, either, if she hadn't been eavesdropping on her brother from the office next to his, hadn't seen them together, hadn't overheard them laughing about her naivete. She'd beaten herself up for being so gullible, then broken off the engagement without explanation.

In retrospect, that might not have been the smartest move, as it may have alerted them to her suspicions. But her skin had crawled at the thought of being with that man for even one more second.

"Though I can't place all of the blame on Lloyd. I'd just left the life I loved behind and moved back to California after being gone for years. I'd lost my father, the only person I was ever really close to. My brother didn't want me there. He forced me to work as a junior analyst, even though everyone knew I was part owner of the company, which left me isolated and alone." She scoffed. "I guess I should have realized Lloyd was too good to be true. But when he told me he could understand my pain, my grief, my sadness because he'd lost his own father, I believed him. I was a fool."

"You weren't a fool, Olivia." Angela reached out and took her hand. "You were just lonely and vulnerable. And Lloyd preyed on your grief, used your loneliness to insinuate himself into your life and gain your trust."

"Thank you for that, for understanding, and for not making me feel even more foolish than I already do." Olivia squeezed Angela's hand, appreciating the gesture of support, and realized she was going to miss this. Somehow, in such a short time, she'd come to think of Zac's team as something more—friends maybe.

"Were he and your brother close friends?"

She considered that. "I don't know if they were friends, but Lloyd is Tristan's right hand in the business, his enforcer, his problem solver."

"And you were a problem?"

She sniffed, nodded and let the tears fall. The heartbreak she felt at his betrayal back then hadn't returned with her memories, though she understood now why trust seemed so difficult for her, even with no memory of her past. Everyone she'd trusted, her brother, her fia—Lloyd, had betrayed her. Even she and Amy weren't all that close if she let herself examine the relationship from a neutral standpoint, considering Amy's petty digs and jealousy over Olivia and their father's close relationship.

But that grief, the sorrow at losing the one man who'd meant everything to her, who would never have hurt her, returned with a vengeance and threatened to swallow her whole. Of all her memories, that was the one that cut the deepest, the one that opened the wound as if he'd only passed away in that moment. She'd already known he was gone, but she hadn't been prepared for the depths of her grief and pain. And anger.

Caleb had suggested her father's death might not have been from natural causes. Surely, he would look into that while he was with Angela and whatever other agents were present.

Still…it was time to tuck her grief back into a small box in the corner of her heart. She'd have plenty of time to revisit it when this was done. For now, it was time to pull up her big girl pants and end this. She'd made a promise to her father after reading his journal that she'd finish his work so he could rest in peace. And she had. It had taken long months away from the home she loved, but she'd succeeded. Now, she finally had the proof she'd been searching for. It was time to stop feeling sorry for herself, take Tristan and Lloyd down and find Amy. "Thank you, Angela."

"Of course. Anytime you need a sounding board, I'm here." With that, Angela stood. "So, are you ready to take them down now?"

"More ready than you could ever know."

Olivia found Caleb, along with Zac, Mason and Chase, huddled around the dining room table. A coffeepot sat close by, folders and papers were scattered across the tabletop, and three laptops sat open.

Caleb jumped to his feet, then stood frozen, seemingly unsure how to handle her. That was okay, considering she had no clue what to do with him, either. So where did that leave them?

Where indeed. That was a problem for another day.

With that in mind, along with the kiss and the feeling of being embraced in Caleb's arms that she was trying so hard to ignore, she simply nodded to him and sat beside Angela.

"Um…" Caleb cleared his throat and started again. "Can I get you a cup of tea?"

She held up a hand. "Thank you, but I'm good."

He nodded, sat and pulled his chair closer to the table, all while avoiding eye contact with her.

That was probably for the best. It was time to distance herself from whatever she might even have been considering with Caleb before her memories returned. She had a mission that took precedence over everything else. And so did he. He'd vowed to save as many people as he could—and that was what she was to him, someone in need of saving.

Well, it was long past time she stopped playing the victim. "Was that call from Lloyd?"

Zac shifted his gaze to Caleb. Everyone else followed suit.

When silence descended, Caleb finally lifted his gaze

from his hands clasped together in a white-knuckled grip atop the table. When he found everyone staring at him, he startled. "Oh, sorry. Um, yes. Lloyd called. He wanted to set up a meeting to get the flash drive from you. Apparently, Tristan didn't buy that you had amnesia. He wants access to his computers and his accounts unlocked by midnight tonight."

"Or else?"

He shrugged and finally met her gaze. The horror reflected there told her all she needed to know.

She shifted in her seat, stiffened her spine. These people, all of them, Caleb included, had already risked more for her than she would have allowed if she'd understood the stakes. They were protectors, defenders, the kind of people you turned to when you were in real trouble. They weren't going to like what she had in mind. But so be it.

"So... I have copies of the financials, communications, the whole paper trail for the money-laundering that took place," Olivia said. "I wrote a code to lock down the company so they couldn't continue with their illegal activities or destroy the evidence if they realized what I did. I intended to turn it all over to the police and let them handle it."

The memory came fierce and unbidden—a gunman opening fire on a crowded street, people fleeing for their lives. The breath exploded from her lungs, her eyes fluttered closed, and she slumped in her seat. How many people had died because of her already? Tremors ripped through her. "There was an incident when I fled..."

Angela gripped her hand and squeezed.

For the instant she allowed herself before shutting it

down, Olivia wished it was Caleb. Caleb, whose strong hand had guided her through this mess. Caleb, who'd saved her, who'd held her, who'd kissed her—who'd been injured for her, who could have been killed because of her.

She forced the words past the lump clogging her throat. "Before anything else, I need to know how many victims there've been since I ran."

"We've already traced your steps back to the day you fled the company. Thankfully, no one was killed, and there were no major injuries," Zac told her.

She nodded and tried to thank him, but her breath caught on a sob.

Caleb set a bottle of water and a box of tissues on the table in front of her, then returned to his seat without saying a word.

She took a moment to collect herself and offer a prayer of thanks that no one had been killed or seriously injured. Once she regained control of her runaway emotions, she began again. "Thank you. All of you. For everything you've done for me. I don't have words to express how grateful I am. Especially, to you, Caleb."

She finally met his gaze and held it, willing him to understand the depths of her gratitude.

He stared back at her, his expression neutral, and nodded once.

"As I started to say, I locked all of the computers at Delaney Investments, locked all of the bank accounts, even the hidden ones, and had planned to turn the evidence over to the police and then return to my life in Florida. I was in a limo—my brother insisted I be driven everywhere, made it seem like it was part of the Delaney lifestyle, but it was really just to track my movements. My driver… He was in on it, I guess. He handed me my sister's picture as proof of life and demanded I hand him the drive. I didn't understand at first. He pulled a gun, and I pulled my pepper spray…"

She would have to live with that, causing the crash even in self-defense.

"Is the company still locked down?" Zac asked.

"Yep," Einstein said. "That was some serious code. They have to insert the flash drive into a company computer if they want to unlock anything. No wonder they're desperate to get it back."

Olivia gritted her teeth. "Tristan may have murdered my father. He came after me and is threatening my sister's life. I will do anything in my power to save Amy. And Tristan and Lloyd are going down. Even if it turns out my father did have a heart attack, and there was no foul play involved there, Tristan's betrayal could have been what pushed him over the edge."

"I've already been in contact with the authorities in California," Zac said.

She glanced up at him.

"Discreetly, of course. I told them I couldn't get into everything just yet, but that we were handling an investigation that led us to believe Malcolm Delaney's death may have been intentional, and they have agreed to work with us to find out."

"Okay. Good." Olivia nodded. "That's good. Thank you."

"You're welcome. Now, why don't you tell us everything you found out, and we can figure out a way to move forward?"

"Thank you, and again, I appreciate all of your help.

But I can't allow you to keep putting your own lives in danger for me."

"We're not doing it for you, Olivia." Zac smiled. "Well, we are, but helping is what we do. At first, we stepped in because Caleb asked for help. Then, I'll admit, we were all intrigued by your case. And now…well, now we're invested and have every intention of seeing this through— with or without your help. Because that's where this is going, right? You want to go back to California and take down Tristan yourself?"

She nodded. "I think it's for the best."

Caleb lurched to his feet, knocking the chair over behind him. "Uh-uh. No way. That is not happening."

She stood and planted her hands on the table. "Look, Caleb—"

"Okay. That's enough." Zac sighed, got to his feet and held his hands out. "Arguing will get us nowhere. Olivia, how about this? You tell us everything you know, we'll decide together on a plan of action that works for you, and then we'll put an end to this. Does that work?"

Did it? She didn't know. She was so confused. About everything. But the one certainty in her mind was that Tristan had to pay for what he'd done. "Okay. Thank you."

"Good."

"But only under one condition," she added.

Caleb muttered something under his breath, then righted his chair and dropped onto it, arms folded across his chest.

"What condition?" Zac asked.

"I will pay Jameson Investigations for your services. It's the only way I'll feel okay about involving all of you.

You said this is what you do, and I understand and appreciate that. So let me hire you to help me investigate this."

"Fair enough. When it's all said and done, I'll send you a bill." Zac winked at Caleb. "I already have a payment plan in mind, but we can see when it's all over."

"Okay, I'll agree to that." Olivia held her hand out to Zac across the table.

He shook her hand and resumed his seat. "Besides, you hiring us jibes with what Caleb told Tristan when they spoke."

"Oh, and what's that?"

Zac gestured for Caleb to expand. Caleb pressed a thumb and forefinger against his eyes for a moment. Olivia could certainly understand his frustration and even sympathize.

"Tristan wanted to know what my involvement was. I told him I was just muscle you hired to keep from getting killed when you realized someone was after you. I think he bought it, since it's probably what he'd do. Plus, I let him go when we were in the swamp, and if I were a police officer, I wouldn't have done so. Unfortunately, he didn't believe you had amnesia. He thinks it's a stalling tactic to buy you time to rescue Amy. Ironic, considering that the amnesia part was actually true."

Olivia spent the next half hour worried sick for Amy as she rehashed what she'd already told Caleb about her return to Delaney Investments, Tristan's drug problem and his rise through the ranks of the cartel. She kept her gaze averted from Caleb when she told the team about Lloyd's role, how she'd accidentally unearthed the scheme he and her brother had concocted to keep her in line. She didn't think she could handle the sympathy she might find in his expression. Or the anger that would mirror her own.

When she was done, she uncapped her water bottle and took a long drink.

"So what do you have in mind?" Zac asked.

"I'm going to return to California, give Tristan the flash drive, and assure him no one knows of its existence. Then I'm going to get my sister back safely and go undercover. It might take me the rest of my life to earn any level of trust again within the company, but I will find a way to bring him down. It will just take time."

Time she was willing to invest in order to see her brother pay for his crimes, for what he'd done to their family, for what he may have done to their father. Even though it meant giving up the life she wanted so badly, her dream of being an artist, her peace that came from living in harmony with nature. None of it mattered without the truth. Hopefully, one day, she'd be able to find happiness again.

"Would you consider a compromise that would allow you to bring him down sooner?" Zac studied a folder as he pointedly avoided making eye contact with anyone, as if it were a casual request rather than a well-thought-out plan.

Olivia wasn't buying it.

Caleb sat up straighter and scowled at Zac.

Zac lowered the folder to the table, stood and clasped his hands in front of him. "You won't have to go to California to confront Tristan. He's here in Florida with Lloyd. And, according to what he told Caleb, they brought Amy as well."

She gasped, caught off guard by the lengths Tristan was willing to go to. She'd assumed he'd sent Lloyd to do his dirty work while he stayed in California keeping his hands clean.

"I'd like you to consider going in wearing a wire," Zac said calmly.

Chaos erupted as Caleb, Mason and Chase all jumped to their feet to argue against the plan.

Angela remained noticeably quiet, not offering her opinion one way or the other.

Olivia patiently waited them out, listened and weighed each of their arguments, both for and against, then slowly got to her feet. "Tell me what I have to do."

Everyone dispersed to set up the operation—Zac and Angela to coordinate with local law enforcement and the FBI, since abducting Amy and taking her across state lines allowed them access. Mason and Chase were charged with checking weapons.

Caleb found Olivia in the living room. She stood staring out the front windows, arms wrapped tightly around herself. Wind whipped the trees into a frenzy, and rain pounded against the windows and roof, nearly drowning out the soft sound of her sobs.

He and Olivia hadn't spoken, other than in a group regarding the coming operation, since he pulled her into his arms and kissed her. He'd spent the past day beating himself up over it, but he couldn't go back and change it, wasn't even sure he would if he was able. There was something about her. There was no denying her beauty, but she had so much more to offer. And now that her memories had returned, and he understood what she'd endured to keep a posthumous promise to her father, he could add loyalty to her list of attributes. And that was a quality that touched him deeper than any other, considering his past experience.

Not wanting to startle her, he cleared his throat to get her attention.

She wiped her cheeks with her sleeves, then looked over her shoulder.

"I'm sorry to bother you, but I want to run through everything one more time."

"Sure." She waved him forward and offered a tentative smile. "If you think the hundred or so times we've already gone over it isn't enough, we could do it again."

He approached her slowly, savoring what might be their last moments together before she went in alone. No matter how hard Caleb argued against it, Zac had ended up agreeing with Olivia that Tristan would be more likely to be open with Olivia on her own. Not that Zac was a dictator. But since all the other agents eventually agreed with Zac and Olivia, Caleb had been outvoted. Besides, if he was being honest with himself, he had to admit he might not be thinking as rationally as the others with his feelings for her all muddled and confusing.

So now, here he stood, awkwardly facing a woman he'd come to care for, though he still couldn't be sure how it had happened. Somehow, the walls he'd erected around his heart had crumbled, failing him when he needed them the most. And where did that leave him? "Before we go over the operation, I owe you an apology."

She frowned. "What for?"

"For kissing you."

Her smile faltered.

"I'm sorry. It was unprofessional, and I don't know how it happened, but I can assure you it won't happen again."

"Don't worry about it. It's fine. It was partly my fault anyway. I…" She shook her head. "Why don't we just forget it ever happened and start over?"

Was that what he wanted? Maybe what he wanted didn't matter. It certainly hadn't when Rachel had walked out on him.

When she stuck out her hand, tears once again shimmered in her eyes. "Friends?"

He took her hand in his, had to resist the urge to pull her into his arms, to protect her, to love her.

Whoa. Love? Could he really come to love Olivia? Given time for them both to heal, could he find it in his heart to love again? He had no idea. It seemed both of them were emotional train wrecks. And now certainly wasn't the time to search for the answer. "Friends."

She nodded and lowered her gaze. One tear tipped over her lashes and rolled down her cheek.

For him? Did she want something more between them? Was he blowing this? And before he knew what was going to come out of his mouth, he started to babble an explanation. "My wife—"

Her gaze shot to his, eyes wide.

"Sorry, ex-wife. Rachel and I were young when we were married. And I had goals, aspirations that went beyond just marriage and a family."

She gripped his hands in hers, squeezed without even seeming to realize it.

He held on tight, as if her hands were a lifeline that would drag him through the telling. "I wanted to dedicate my life to helping people, to saving as many as I could. First, I spent time in the service, then I returned home and went to work for the FBI. So I guess I have to shoulder part of the blame for what happened."

"What did happen, if you don't mind me asking?"

"She had an affair. With my best friend. I suppose it was partly my fault for not being there for her more often."

Olivia tugged his hands. "If you ask me, it sounds like she was being kind of selfish. It's not like you were out partying or something. You were trying to do something good with your life, to follow the plan God laid out for you."

A smile tugged at him, and the knot of tension in his gut began to unravel. "If only Rachel had been so understanding. But she was young, and she had desires and goals of her own that I didn't live up to."

Olivia released his hands and hugged him, just a friendly squeeze to offer support, then she stepped back.

"Anyway, when she told me she was pregnant, I promised all of that would change. I told her I would take a job with local law enforcement, so I'd be closer to home more often." The pain of losing the child he'd thought was his cut too deep. He wanted desperately to clamp his mouth shut and walk away. But Olivia deserved the truth. All of it. So… "She told me not to bother. She was leaving me, moving in with my best friend—the baby's real father."

"Oh, Caleb. I'm so sorry. That must have been awful."

"It was one of the worst days of my life. It was as if all the joy was sucked out of me." He'd questioned God then, had lost his faith for just a moment. But then another opportunity presented itself. "I wandered for a while, lost, alone, angry. And then I ran into Zac Jameson in a bar one night. To this day, I wonder if Zac facilitated that meeting, if he sought me out, though every time I ask him, all he does is smile and remind me God works in mysterious ways, and often we are right where we are meant to be at the exact moment we're supposed to be there."

Her grin went straight to his heart. "Zac's a smart guy."

"Yeah." And with that, the grief in his heart lightened. "Yeah, he is. Anyway, I just wanted you to know that I understand betrayal. I understand how badly it hurts, how much it affects our ability to trust again. And I'm sorry I led you to believe there might be anything other than friendship between us. I don't know what came over me in that moment, but—"

"Don't worry about it, Caleb. I was there, too, and a willing participant. Why don't we just chalk it up to the heat of the moment? Both of us were in pain and scared. And who knows? Maybe we each recognized a kindred spirit in the other and reached toward each other in a moment of weakness."

He nodded, thankful she understood, especially when her life might depend on her trusting him. "I promise you, Olivia, I will have your back. You are not alone, and we will not abandon you."

"Thank you for that, Caleb."

"Sure." He let it go at that, even though his heart begged him to say so much more. He wanted to plead with her not to go through with this, to hide her away and keep her safe. But he understood that his path lay in his work, not in another failed attempt at a relationship. And Olivia's path led to taking down her brother. He would not deny her that, refused to interfere with her keeping the promise she'd made to her father and was so determined to uphold.

"Okay, then. Want to go over the plan?"

Boy, did he. Planning for every eventuality in an op was so much easier than navigating the depth of feelings he couldn't begin to understand. "Absolutely."

He led her to the dining room table, shuffled through a stack of folders, then stood beside her. Neither of them bothered to sit. He was too hyped up, and he recognized the signs in her as well.

"Don't forget, your phone is a listening device and a GPS locator, so try to keep it with you at all times. You don't have to take it out. Just leave it in your pocket, and we'll do the rest. And even if they take it from you, it won't matter as long as they keep it nearby. If they suspect anything and destroy the phone, the locket Angela gave you contains a backup listening device. And if you're forced to go on the run without the phone, just leave it behind and go. The tracking device in your locket will allow us to find you even if we can't communicate with you."

She nodded. "It certainly seems you've covered every contingency."

Everything they could think of, at least, but there was always the unexpected. They'd considered sending her in with a traditional wire, but Tristan was a high-ranking member of a massive international drug cartel. He laundered money for some of the worst criminals on the FBI's most wanted list. He had not reached that position by being careless. If they found a wire when they searched her, which they no doubt would, she wouldn't last long enough for Zac's team to break the door down and get to her. "You remember the code phrase for if you get in trouble, right?"

"Yeah." She chuckled. "I look Tristan dead in the eye and ask him how he became such a monster."

He couldn't help but laugh. The code phrase had been her idea. She'd insisted if she was going out, she refused to do so without letting her brother know exactly what she thought of him.

The thought was like a bucket of ice water tossed in Caleb's face.

He sucked in a deep breath and averted his gaze, then opened the top folder and pulled out a map and a blueprint of the building where they were set to meet. The fact that his hands shook was no doubt due to adrenaline. "Angela was able to pull these up. I need you to look them over and memorize them. Can you do that?"

She nodded and got to work. She surveyed the documents, all signs of the vulnerable woman he'd found silhouetted by the raging storm only an hour ago gone. "What exactly am I looking at?"

He pointed to the map first. "This is the house you're set to meet at. Tristan knows you'll have bodyguards nearby but have agreed to meet with him alone as a token of good faith. It's a two-story building in a remote area of the swamp not far from your cabin, which would be over here."

She tapped a spot on the table where her cabin would be situated if the map were bigger. "Okay. I know this area. This is actually good. I've spent a tremendous amount of time in these woods, traversed the swamp for my paintings and my own enjoyment."

"Would you be comfortable enough to go on the run if you had to?"

"Yeah."

"Even in the dark?"

She swallowed hard and examined every inch of the

map. "Yes. I could figure out how to get back to my cabin from here. But it would mean hiking through the swamp for at least five or six miles, alone, in the pitch-black."

"Nine point three miles to be exact. Hopefully, it won't come to that. But I don't want you feeling trapped. Zac's agents, along with FBI and local authorities, will be surrounding the house but at a distance so Tristan's thugs won't see us. If anything goes wrong, we'll intervene immediately, but it will take a moment for us to get there. If you feel like things are going south, you have to promise me you'll abandon the plan and bail." He tapped a door at the back of the house on the blueprint. "This door would allow you to get out and into the cover of the trees the quickest. If you head to your right, you'll be on a direct path toward your cabin."

She shifted the map, tilted her head, then studied it beside the blueprint. "What about this side door? It would take an extra minute or two to reach the woods, but a road runs right behind them here."

He and Zac had already discussed and dismissed that option. "Only do that if you have no choice. One, we want you hidden from view as soon as possible. And two, that road is exactly where he'd expect you to go, and we all agree he'll have men stationed there."

She chewed her lip and nodded.

"Olivia." He propped a finger beneath her chin and tilted her head to face him. "You don't have to do this. I can go in for you. I *want* to go in in your place."

"No. Thank you, Caleb, really, but I have to do this. Most of all, we need to find Amy, and I have the best chance at getting him to release her."

She also ran the highest risk of Tristan killing her. And Amy.

"But I need you to make me a promise. Please," she added.

If I can. Because he knew better than to make a blind promise on an op that he might not be able to keep. There were no certainties in this situation, only bad and worse possible outcomes. "What do you need me to do?"

"Promise me that no matter what happens to me, you'll find Amy and get her out of there. Please, promise me that, Caleb. She's an innocent bystander in all of this. I was the one who stuck my nose into Tristan's business, and it's not fair that she is paying the price for that."

He swallowed the lump of fear clogging his throat and nodded. "I'll do my best. I promise you that."

"That's all I can ask. Thank you."

"You bet." He reached for her then, cradled her cheek in his hand, studied every inch of her features.

She covered his hand with her own, weaved her fingers between his and tilted her face into their joined hands. "We'll get him, Caleb. And after we do, I think I'm going to try your idea of going off grid for a while. I'll return to my cabin, spend some time with Amy, help her heal and get through whatever pain she's suffered from this ordeal. And then I'm going to step away. I don't know where yet, but somewhere peaceful and quiet."

Seeming to sense her need, Ranger stood and nudged her hand with his head.

She petted his head, ran her hand down his back and beamed. "And before I do that, I'm going to the shelter to get myself a dog to share my journey with. Unless you'd be willing to give up Ranger for me."

"Not for anything." *Not even you.*

She gazed down at the big dog, her expression soft and filled with love, and he looked up at her the same way. "I can't blame you."

A knock against the wall broke the connection. Angela poked her head into the room. "It's time."

TEN

Olivia wiped her sweaty palms on her leggings before she climbed out of the SUV Zac had lent her. She started up the pathway to the two-story plantation-style house surrounded by a small clearing. She resisted the urge to look over her shoulder. It would do no good, and she'd been warned not to. All of Zac's agents were posted too far away for her to see, but knowing they were there helped.

Knowing Caleb was there helped. She hadn't expected to be so frightened when the time came. And now, she just wanted to get through the next little while and put all this behind her. Caleb, too? She had no idea. But she couldn't think about him now. She had to focus, or there was a better than good chance someone would get killed.

Her Keds hit the pavers softly, yet her footsteps seemed loud in the silence, a stark reminder that she was alone. Except, she wasn't. She'd never be alone.

God, please help me through these next few moments. Please help me to find my sister and save her. Help me put an end to Tristan's reign of terror. Please watch over and protect all of the agents trying to stop Tristan and protect me. And, please, watch over Caleb and Ranger, who have already risked and suffered so much to keep me safe.

Two men with very large weapons emerged from the house, trotted down the front steps and bracketed her.

She continued up the walkway without acknowledging their presence. Holding her breath, she ascended the three front steps and walked into a well-appointed foyer. She only released her breath when the door shut behind her and locked with a resounding click.

The aroma of potpourri hit her, thick and cloying, and she couldn't help but wonder what kind of odor they might be trying to hide. She swallowed, the scent sticking in the back of her throat.

When the two gunmen made no move to take her any farther into the luxurious home, Olivia took a moment to situate herself. Curved stairways led up from either side of the foyer, a balcony between them offering a perfect view of the elaborate crystal chandelier overhead. Though she already knew the layout, the blueprints hadn't prepared her for the sheer opulence. Gaudy marble flooring with streams of gold running through it and an elaborate gold circle design in its center, gold fixtures and doorknobs and freestanding artwork that, while no doubt expensive, seemed garish and pretentious.

Angela had said Tristan built the house years ago, and the style suited him well—cold. The fact that he'd maintained a home so close to her own for years turned her stomach.

Footsteps alerted Olivia to someone's approach, and she quickly surveyed the rest of the area to get her bearings.

"Well, well, well." Lloyd leaned a shoulder against the foyer wall, stuffed his hands in the pockets of his Dockers and crossed one foot over the other. "If it isn't my long lost fiancée."

"I'm not your fiancée, Lloyd. As a matter of fact, you're nothing to me at all. Now, where is Tristan?"

"All in good time, Olivia. But first…" He nodded toward one of the gunmen and leered at her. His gaze traveling up and down her body sent a chill up her spine, but he waited while the guy patted her down. "I'd have done that myself, but full disclosure, I don't trust you not to put a bullet in my head if I get too close—even if Tristan does."

She said nothing, simply held his gaze while one guy covered her, the other checked her for weapons, and Lloyd lounged against the wall. When she agreed to meet with Tristan, she'd hoped Lloyd would be outside somewhere watching for trouble. Not that it would have made a difference. She'd still have come. But she would prefer to deal only with Tristan.

Her heart rate accelerated, sweat beaded her temples and ran down her hairline, and ice-cold dread gripped her heart.

"Actually, now that I think of it, I don't think Tristan really trusts you so much as underestimates you. But I don't, Olivia. Not for a minute." He glanced at the gunman who'd frisked her.

He stepped back and nodded.

Lloyd approached, contemplating her as he walked a tight circle around her.

She worked to keep her breathing steady, desperate to appear unfazed by his scrutiny. *God, help me. I think I might have gotten in over my head here.*

Then something settled within her, a sense of peace. For so many long months, she'd lived a lie in order to save her father's company from Tristan's betrayal. And in probably less than an hour, it would all be over. One way or another.

She inhaled deeply. The potpourri and another odor

invaded her senses, something horrid, decaying. In some corner of her mind, she recognized the smell of death from her numerous excursions through the swamp. Her heart skipped a beat. "Where is Amy?"

"All in good time, dear." Lloyd stopped facing her and smirked, then held out his hand.

One of the gunmen handed him a small electronic device.

He turned it on and ran it over Olivia's body, stopping when he came to the pocket of her windbreaker. He held her gaze, his eyes going almost black, predatory. "Tsk, tsk, tsk, Olivia."

He pointed to the gunman, then to Olivia.

The guy pulled her phone from her pocket, dropped it onto the hard marble floor and crushed it beneath his combat boot.

She gasped, sheer terror washing over her, then tried to cover her reaction. "Hey, what was that for?"

"Do you take me for a fool, Olivia? Do you think everyone is as gullible as you are?"

Apparently, they had some sort of equipment sophisticated enough to detect the surveillance. It didn't matter, though. Caleb had assured her the phone would still work to pick up the conversation, and if it didn't, the device in the locket would. She briefly considered uttering the code they'd agreed upon, then dismissed the thought just as quickly.

So far, these men hadn't done anything illegal. Weapons were legal in Florida, and they hadn't used them to threaten her. She seriously doubted crushing her cell phone would get anyone more than a slap on the wrist, and then only the gunman who'd stepped on it. No, she needed more time, needed proof that would put her brother and Lloyd away for a long time.

She closed her eyes and prayed he would be content with what he'd found and not continue his search. Then she opened them, smiled at him and winked. "Can't blame a girl for trying."

Lloyd studied her for a moment, then laughed out loud and handed the device back to the gunman. "You know what, Olivia? I actually have more respect for you for trying. Maybe when all is said and done, we can rekindle our relationship. You and I could make an amazing team. Who knows? Together, we might even be able to overthrow your brother and run the company ourselves."

The fact that he said that out loud made her believe the gunmen currently present must belong to him and not Tristan. She highly doubted Tristan had gotten where he was by tolerating any sort of disloyalty.

Something twisted in her gut, but she'd play along with him for the moment, if it got her closer to Tristan and, more important, to Amy. "I have no idea what the future might hold, Lloyd, but right now, I just want to hand over the flash drive, make amends with my brother and walk out of here with my sister."

"If that's the case, why come in here with a listening device?"

"So my bodyguard can keep track of my movements." She shot him a scathing scowl. "You don't think I'm stupid enough to trust you and Tristan without having a backup plan in place, do you?"

"No. No, I suppose not." He waved the gunmen off, then grabbed her by the arm and yanked her forward.

The two men walked out the front door. Hopefully, Caleb and his team would pick them up.

Lloyd guided her roughly through the house, which seemed to be empty but for the two of them. Where was all their security? Surely, they had some other security in place besides the two gunmen he'd dismissed.

As they passed an open doorway, Olivia turned her head to look across a large study to the back door she was supposed to flee through if the need arose. Her gaze caught on a body in the middle of the floor.

Lloyd leaned close to her ear, his breath brushing her neck. "A competitor. And a reminder to you about what's at stake."

Tremors tore through her, impossible to control, as she offered a prayer for whoever had been killed to provide an example for her.

Lloyd laughed, clearly enjoying tormenting her. When they reached the end of a long hallway, he released her, pushed open a set of double doors and shoved her through.

Tristan sat behind a vast mahogany desk, an imposing figure dressed in a light gray silk suit and black tie, exactly how she remembered him. He didn't bother to stand when she entered.

Tired of the whole charade and anxious to be done and out of there, she strode across the room purposefully, pulled the flash drive from her pocket and slapped it in the center of his cleared blotter. Zac and Angela had worked with their FBI contacts to copy the information from the flash drive, and warrants had been hastily obtained that afternoon for the FBI to search Delaney Investments based on that evidence. All that remained was for Tristan to insert the flash drive into a company computer, and Olivia's encryption key would unlock all of Delaney Investments's files and bank accounts. And then the FBI would swoop in.

"I'm done, Tristan. I just want out. There's the flash drive, now just give me Amy, and I'll be on my way."

He lifted a brow, his ice-cold smile enough to stop her heart. "I don't think so."

"I'm not playing, Tristan. I don't want any part of this." Then she remembered Caleb telling her to play to his ego, to appear weak and fragile, to catch him off guard. She took a step back and lowered her gaze, clasped her hands in front of her and fidgeted her fingers. "Please, Tristan. I just want to take Amy and go home. I'll leave the company and stay in Florida. I'd prefer to be here anyway."

"To live in the forest like some kind of swamp rat?"

She firmed her lips and said nothing.

"I don't think so. I think maybe I'd like you to return to California, continue to work for Delaney Investments and marry Lloyd here, so we can keep an eye on you."

She gasped but resisted every instinct begging her to lunge over the desk and punch him, and nodded demurely. "Whatever you say, Tristan. But can I please see Amy?"

He narrowed his eyes, suspicion darkening the gaze that lingered on her, then he lifted his chin toward Lloyd, who gritted his teeth and walked out. It seemed all might not be well in paradise. Something to keep in mind in case they could turn Lloyd against him. For now, though...

As soon as she had Amy, Zac's team would move in. But she hadn't managed to get any sort of confession from Tristan. And while a confession would help shore up the evidence of his illegal activities contained on the flash drive in Angela's possession, there was something more pressing on her mind. She didn't even realize what she was going to ask before the question quietly emerged.

She didn't have to fake the tremor in her voice. "Did you kill our father, Tristan?"

A slow grin spread across his face. He stood, walked slowly toward her, caging her gaze with his own. When he reached her, he leaned close, his breath hot against her. "Of course I did."

The scream welled from somewhere deep within her, and a year's worth of pain and grief emerged when it let loose.

But he simply threw his head back and laughed.

She swung blindly, raking her nails across his cheek. "If it's the last thing I do, I will see to it that you pay for that. He was a good man. He never deserved you for a son."

"Maybe not." He shrugged, took a handkerchief from his pocket and dabbed the blood welling on his cheek. "But we all take the cards we're dealt."

Lloyd returned then, with Amy in tow, putting an end to their conversation.

She had nothing left to say to Tristan anyway. Nor did she have any interest in hearing whatever he might say. She only prayed Caleb had recorded his confession, and Tristan would spend the rest of his life rotting in jail and contemplating the man he'd taken everything from. Right now, her concern had to be for her sister, who could still be saved.

Amy's hands were bound in front of her, her expression dazed. When Lloyd shoved her toward Olivia, she stumbled but regained her balance.

Relief weakened Olivia's knees, and she almost went down. Sheer willpower kept her on her feet. She didn't bother trying to contain the sob as she ran to her sister and threw her arms around her neck. "Are you okay, Amy? Are you hurt? I'm so sorry."

"Okay, enough of this." Tristan yanked Amy away from her and shoved her toward the desk.

Amy's hip connected hard with the wood, and she cried out.

He pulled out a handgun and gestured toward Lloyd before grabbing Olivia by the arm and shoving her toward the back of the room. "Take all her jewelry, and let's go."

"Go where?" Olivia blurted. "What are you talking about? I gave you what you wanted, and you promised you'd let us go."

"Yeah, well, plans change."

Lloyd removed her watch and her earrings. When he grabbed her locket, she splayed a hand over it. "Please, Tristan, let me keep this. It's not worth anything, but Dad gave it to me, and it has a lot of sentimental value."

Tristan eyed her for a few seconds and walked over to face her. "You'd be shocked at how much technology can be hidden in something that small. No need for anyone to track us, is there?"

When she looked into his eyes, she saw nothing. They were like dark wells with no emotion, no feeling, no love. Nothing but two black pits. She knew in that instant exactly what he had planned. He had terrorized her, and now he would kill her.

Why hadn't she listened to Caleb? Why had she insisted she could confront her brother? She'd hoped to save Amy, but now it looked like Amy would die with her. She'd failed her sister. She'd failed her father. Pain squeezed her heart.

And she'd failed Caleb. She should have told him the

truth, should have shared the depth of her feelings for him when she had the chance. And now she would die without ever getting the opportunity to tell him how she really felt about him.

Tristan reached out and grabbed her locket, then ripped it from her neck.

She didn't bother holding back the tears. "What happened to you, Tristan? How did you become such a monster?"

He held her stare and grinned as he crushed the locket beneath his shoe.

"Go! Go! Go!" Zac's voice boomed through Caleb's earpiece, but it was Olivia's words that still echoed in his head, and the fear he heard there when she uttered the code phrase.

"Ranger, find!" Caleb held one of Olivia's shirts out for the dog to scent, then jumped out the back of the electric company truck they'd borrowed and ran with Ranger at his side. They should have gone in sooner, had started to after his confession, but couldn't until they knew Amy was on scene. They'd hoped Tristan would allow Olivia to walk out with her sister, and they could go in and take him down with the two women out of harm's way.

Footsteps pounded, voices chattered, and Caleb searched for calm as Zac's agents and law enforcement officials converged on the scene. This was an op, just like any other. Emotions had no place here, nor did—

An explosion rocked the night, the massive fireball lifting him off his feet. He hit the ground hard and rolled, his head smacking the pavement.

Ranger tumbled beside him, then regained his footing, splayed his feet and started to bark.

Caleb opened his eyes, struggled to sit up, to even understand which way was up. All sound was muffled to a dull roar. The world seemed to move in slow motion around him, carrying on though he was somehow paused in that moment.

"Caleb!" The word seemed familiar, coming to him from a great distance or underwater, maybe.

Where was he? He struggled to focus. For an instant there was nothing, and then it all crashed back over him, a tidal wave he had no hope of escaping. *Olivia!*

"Caleb! Hey, man, you hurt?" Zac crouched beside him, weapon cradled in his arm. "Hey! Can you hear me? Are you hurt?"

What had he done? How could he have agreed to let her go in alone? But as he watched Tristan's house burn, that wasn't the real question haunting him. How could he have let her go in without telling her how he felt about her, without being honest with himself, if not her, about how much he'd come to care for her? He should have told her he was willing to risk his heart to see if they could make something together. And now the chance was gone.

"Caleb. On your feet. We need to move back." Zac scooped one hand beneath his arm and helped him to stand.

"Ranger?"

"He's here, man. He's fine."

"Olivia?" Caleb started to cough, pain squeezing his chest.

"We don't know yet. We need to fall back, regroup."

Sirens screamed through the night, the strobe effects

from the converging emergency vehicles dizzying. "She was at the back of the house."

"I know. Mason and Chase are already on their way back there."

Caleb narrowed his gaze, worked to bring his vision back into focus. "Are they hurt?"

Zac shook his head. "They were behind you when the house went up."

"The others?"

"Chatter has at least three officers and one FBI agent down."

Caleb sucked in a deep breath that burned all the way to his lungs as he prayed they would all make it, prayed Olivia had somehow managed to survive, even if he saw no way. "I have to know, Zac."

Zac nodded. "I know. Just take a second to get your bearings, and we'll go find her."

Caleb didn't need a second; he needed Olivia, needed to find her, to apologize and confess how much he cared for her. Then, if she decided to walk away, he'd live with it. At least he would know she was safe.

He staggered a step forward, and Zac reached out to steady him.

"I'm all right. I just have to find her, Zac. No matter what."

Zac patted his shoulder. "I know."

As Caleb rounded the house with Zac and Ranger, his steps steadied. *Lord, please have saved her somehow.*

The instant he spotted Mason and Chase behind the house, their dire expressions illuminated by the flames, his hope died. When he reached them, Mason shook his head. "I'm sorry, man. There's just no way in. The house, the garden, everything went up."

Caleb simply nodded. What could he say? He had no doubt at all if there was a way into that building, Mason and Chase would have entered, despite any risk to themselves. He flopped onto a wrought iron bench, propped his elbows on his knees and cradled his pounding head in his hands. What-ifs hounded him.

Ranger stood at alert beside the bench.

In the chaos, Caleb had forgotten to remove his vest, forgotten he'd issued the command to find Olivia, and Ranger would remain in work mode until he succeeded. As Caleb reached for him, Ranger stiffened.

He lifted his nose in the air and sniffed, then turned in a circle, seemingly confused.

"Ranger?" Was something wrong with him? Had he been injured in the explosion?

Then his entire body went rigid, his hackles rose, and he started to bark and took off.

Caleb went after him, with Mason, Chase and Zac on his heels. He followed Ranger through a wall of hedges on the edge of the property.

Ranger stopped and pawed at the ground, frantically digging in the dirt, then stilled, barked and headed deeper into the swamp, away from the house.

Was it possible Olivia had escaped? Had she gone on the run as they discussed earlier?

"I'll see what he was pawing at here." Zac stopped. "You guys go."

While Caleb ran through the swamp after Ranger, dodging branches, leaping fallen logs and splashing through stagnant water, he monitored the comms.

Zac called for help, then reached out a few moments later. "Caleb, keep your head up out there. You may have company. Ranger unearthed a trapdoor. When we dug it up, we found a tunnel that led from the house to the edge of the property. There's another exit at the edge of the swamp, and that trapdoor stood open."

Hope flared brighter than the flames he'd left behind. *Olivia.*

"I have a chopper in the air, ETA ten minutes, and I'm sending reinforcements."

"Ten–four." Caleb dug deep and increased his pace. They had to find her before Tristan or Lloyd could eliminate her and Amy. *If* Tristan and Lloyd had both escaped the explosion, and *if* they still had both Olivia and Amy in tow. Caleb assumed they at least had Olivia, because Ranger was still tracking the scent Caleb gave him, but he had no idea who else they might have with them. For all Caleb knew, he could be leading his friends into an ambush.

He stopped and issued a short, sharp whistle, calling Ranger back to him.

"What's up?" Mason turned off his flashlight.

Chase followed suit. "You hear something?"

Caleb shook his head. "Not yet, but for all we know, Tristan might have an army out here waiting to eliminate anyone who comes after them. We need to move slower, use a little caution." No matter how badly he wanted to plow full steam ahead. It wouldn't do Olivia any good if Tristan's goons took down the only team who could make it in time to save her and Amy.

"Agreed," Mason said. "Split up."

Caleb stayed the course with Ranger close, still tracking Olivia, while Mason and Chase fanned out to flank them. He listened to the sounds of the night, searching for anything out of the ordinary: a motor starting, gunshots, shovels hitting the moist ground. If he was walking into an ambush, he'd probably never hear a thing. Most predators in the swamp, humans included, would attack in silence, without any warning.

A birdcall, not one native to Florida but one of many signals Jameson Investigations agents used to communicate, was his first clue that Mason or Chase had found something.

"Ranger, stop," Caleb said quietly.

Ranger stilled at his side.

Caleb crept forward, weapon ready, breathing shallow. Keeping low, he studied the terrain. Silence descended, heightening his senses.

"Look out, Cal—" Olivia's call cut off.

And gunfire shattered the night.

"Down!" Caleb dove into the knee-high swamp grass.

Ranger dropped beside him.

Together, they belly crawled toward the shooters—two, by Caleb's count. It had to be Tristan and Lloyd. And now, Caleb had the advantage. He was low, below their line of sight, and he'd been able to locate them when they opened fire. Plus, he had Mason and Chase flanking them. If Tristan and Lloyd were alone, they'd be able to take them.

He eased through the swamp, listening for any sound. Hoping to hear Olivia's voice again. Olivia and Amy were his two disadvantages. In the darkness, he couldn't open fire without being certain of where they were. He'd have to take Tristan and Lloyd down without a weapon. Somehow, that suited him just fine.

Caleb and Ranger inched closer. When they reached the edge of a small clearing, Caleb stopped. He could see the two men silhouetted in the moonlight. There was no sign of Olivia or Amy.

Ranger gathered his back legs beneath him, crouched and readied to spring at Caleb's signal.

Caleb moved slowly, careful not to draw the attention of the two men. He pressed his back against a large oak, using it for cover, and stood. He held his breath as he peered around the corner. Tristan stood only a few feet from him, sweeping the woods with his weapon. Lloyd was about four feet farther past him. Clearly, the two didn't know the swamp well, or they'd have taken cover rather than standing out in the open, backlit by the moon. Foolish, especially when Caleb might not be the only thing stalking them through the swamp.

Unless it was a trap. He hesitated. For all he knew, they had the entire clearing surrounded. He closed his eyes, listened, inhaled deeply. No. There would have been some indication if they had other men out there. He was fairly certain they'd fled alone with the two women, probably intent on meeting up with someone at the road, since that was the direction they'd gone. But they hadn't counted on a K9 team already on scene. They'd expected to sneak out through the tunnel with the explosion as a distraction and disappear into the night with no one the wiser.

A turkey vulture's low, guttural hiss sounded from nearby.

A slow smile spread across his face. Turkey vultures didn't hunt at night. Mason and Chase were in position to back him up. He curled his fists, prayed for patience and waited for Tristan to turn toward him, away from Lloyd.

Then he gave Ranger the hand signal to catch and hold Lloyd.

Ranger launched himself into the clearing and gripped Lloyd's wrist in his teeth.

Caught off guard, Lloyd screamed.

Tristan whirled toward him and lifted his weapon.

Caleb tackled him from behind, knocked him to the ground and went down with him. They rolled in the rancid muck, Caleb frantically trying to get a good hold on Tristan's slick gun hand.

"Freeze, Wellington!" Mason yelled. "Don't move."

Ranger growled deep in his throat.

"He won't let go until you drop the weapon and stop struggling," Chase added.

With everyone else's attention on Ranger and Lloyd, Caleb yanked his full focus back to Tristan. He swung his elbow back and caught Tristan in the sternum.

Tristan grunted, wheezed and lost his hold on the weapon.

Caleb took advantage of the moment, rolled and gained his footing. He planted a knee in Tristan's back, pinning him to the ground, and yanked one arm behind him. "Don't move."

"You really think you can stop me?" Tristan laughed. "I'll let you in on a little secret. Now, instead of killing her quickly, I'm going to take my sweet time."

Ignoring the taunt, resisting the urge to punch him again, Caleb clenched his teeth, then pulled out his cuffs and first cuffed one wrist and then the other behind Tristan's back. Then he stood and gripped Tristan beneath his arm. "Let's go, Tristan. On your feet."

He spotted Olivia sitting on a downed log beside Amy

with Ranger at her side, still in protection mode as he stood at alert. In the darkness, he couldn't make out her features or her expression, but she was alive and conscious. That would have to be enough for now.

"I've got him, Caleb." Chase took over wrestling Tristan out of the clearing behind Mason and Lloyd.

With both of them in custody, Caleb started toward Olivia, his heart in his throat.

She stood when she saw him coming and took a step toward him.

Amy jumped to her feet behind her. Before Olivia could take a second step, Amy grabbed her in a choke hold from behind. She held a gun against Olivia's temple. "Take one more step, buddy, and I end her."

Ranger crouched.

"No! Ranger, stay."

"Amy?" Olivia tried to turn her head toward her sister, but Amy pressed the gun tighter.

"Don't move and don't say another word."

"I don't understand. You're in on this?"

"Of course I am. How could I attain a top spot in the company without knowing what was going on?" Amy scoffed. "We're not all as sweet and innocent as you, you know. And not all of us had Daddy wrapped around our little fingers."

"Is that what this is about? Some petty childhood jealousy?"

Amy smacked Olivia on the side of the head with the gun.

Caleb lunged.

Amy pointed the weapon at him and fired without warning.

Pain radiated through his shoulder, and he lurched sideways as Ranger attacked. The German shepherd grabbed her wrist between his teeth and shook his head back and forth, growling wildly as he did.

Olivia whirled and caught Amy with an uppercut that staggered her, and she lost her grip on the weapon. Kicking it aside as she moved, Olivia ran to Caleb just as Zac and two other agents entered the clearing.

"Ranger, release."

The big dog let go instantly and returned to Caleb while Zac and his men took Amy into custody.

"Are you all right?" Caleb pulled Olivia into his arms and held her tight, relishing the feeling of how perfectly she fit against him. Once he caught his breath, he pulled back, smoothed her hair out of her face and cradled her face between his hands. "I'm so sorry, Olivia."

"Sorry?" She frowned and shook her head. "For what?"

"I should have told you before how I felt about you. I shouldn't have let the past dictate how I acted. I care more about you than I was willing to admit, even to myself, and I was terrified I'd lose you before I got the chance to tell you the truth."

"I care about you, too, Caleb. Way more than I was ready to admit as well. When Amy shot you, and I knew you'd been hit, my heart stopped completely. I couldn't imagine having to walk out of this clearing without you. I don't know how I would have done it. I don't think I could have."

"I think you could do anything you set your mind to, Olivia. But that said, you're not going anywhere without me for a long while." And he meant that. He had no idea how they were going to pull it off, but he wasn't letting her out of his sight until the shock of seeing that building explode, knowing she was inside, wore off. If it ever did.

She smiled then.

This time he knew exactly who leaned in when he pressed his lips against hers and vowed not to let her out of his arms for quite some time. He didn't know how they were going to work things out between them, with him living in New York and traveling for Jameson Investigations, but he did know they would find a way. Because there was no way he was losing her again.

As more agents began to fill the clearing, he finally stepped back. But he slung an arm around her shoulder and kept her close. "I think we're going to need medical attention."

She winced and gingerly pressed her fingers against her head. "I think you might be right."

He started toward the far side of the clearing. "You hungry?"

She shrugged against him and grinned. "I could eat."

Zac met them partway across the clearing, then simply looked them over and shook his head. Then he handed Olivia a folded piece of paper. "You two all right?"

"Not too bad, all things considered." She glanced down at the page. "What's this?"

"Your bill. And the payment plan I came up with." Zac shined a flashlight on the page.

She opened her mouth to say something, then snapped it closed just as quickly and opened the paper. She read the two words written on it and frowned. "One month? I don't understand."

"You handled yourself well tonight, Olivia, and I can always use an analyst, especially one who's also adept at coding. I want you to come to work for Jameson Investigations for one month, right here in Florida, though it might involve some travel. If you love it, I'd like you to stay on. If not, your debt is paid." He spread his hands and grinned. "What do you say?"

She looked at Caleb, and a wide smile spread across her face. "I'm in."

EPILOGUE

Olivia looked out over the mountains, the view from the ridge incredible. It was hard to believe a year had passed already, and she still choked up whenever she remembered the sound of Amy's gun going off, the sight of Caleb staggering. She paused, uncapped her water bottle and let the cool water ease the ache in her throat.

"You okay?" Caleb studied her and frowned.

She smiled, not only to reassure him but because she was truly happy. The happiest she'd been in as long as she could remember, which, thankfully, was all of her life. "I'm great."

There was no need to explain the pain or fear that returned at random moments; she'd seen the same faraway look in his eyes often enough to know he still suffered with his own memories. But together, they'd begun to heal. Together, they'd learned to trust again—at least, each other. And, when Olivia had completed her training with Zac Jameson, he'd partnered her with Caleb and Ranger, technical backup on most of their missions.

"You want to camp here for the night?"

She looked around the small clearing amid towering redwoods and unshouldered her backpack. "It's perfect."

"I'll gather some firewood, but before I do…" He took her hands in his and kissed her, gently at first and then more passionately.

Heat flared in her cheeks when he pulled away.

"Are you enjoying yourself?"

She grinned. "As far as honeymoons go, this is amazing."

"Thank you, Mrs. Miller."

They'd only been married for three days, but she doubted she'd ever get tired of hearing him call her that. She turned and wrapped an arm around his waist, leaning against him, and watched the sun begin to dip into the valleys.

Ranger nudged her hand, and she petted his head. "You spoke to Zac before when we stopped for a break, but you never told me what he said."

"Are you sure you want to know?"

Did she? She'd mostly avoided asking questions about what happened to Tristan and Amy. It took nearly a year in and out of court, but once Olivia and Caleb had both finished their testimonies, they got married in a small ceremony with a few friends from Jameson Investigations present and then headed off the grid. Olivia had told Caleb to choose their honeymoon destination, anywhere in the world he liked as long as it was somewhere isolated and peaceful. As she looked out over the view, she figured he'd hit it perfectly.

She'd sold Delaney Investments and deposited both Tristan and Amy's shares into accounts for them should they ever get out of prison, then sold the land in California where her house had once stood. "If you know anything, I think I'd like some closure. And then I don't want to think about any of that anymore."

She would still hold the memories somewhere in her mind, because she'd learned that even bad memories were important. If nothing else, for the lessons you learned from them. But she could keep them tucked away where she didn't have to face them all the time.

"Okay, then." He pulled her tighter against him.

She held her breath.

"Tristan was convicted of first-degree murder in your father's death, among other things. He hasn't been sentenced yet, but he's going away for a very long time, probably for the rest of his life."

She nodded, too choked up to speak. It was a bittersweet moment. He'd tormented her for most of her life, he'd lied, cheated, stolen from and betrayed his family, and he'd murdered her father, whom she'd loved with all of her heart. But he was still her brother.

Still, while she felt sad for the boy he might once have been, she couldn't deny feeling safer knowing he'd spend the rest of his life behind bars. And even though she had decided against taking over Delaney Investments, at least she'd gotten justice for her father. She could only pray Tristan would come to realize the mistakes he'd made and try to atone.

"And Lloyd is also going down for first-degree murder for the rival drug dealer he killed in Florida and left in the house they blew up. Zac said they were able to recover enough to match the bullets used to the gun Lloyd had in his possession when he was arrested."

She simply nodded. "And Amy?"

"She was convicted last week for conspiracy to commit murder for her part in procuring the drugs used to kill your father."

And Olivia would continue to pray for her. Finding out Amy had been involved with the drug cartel and money laundering schemes had been bad enough. The knowledge that she'd also been involved in their father's death had left Olivia shaken and shocked. "So that's it? It's done."

"Except for sentencing, it's all over." He hugged her close. "Now, what do you say we set up camp and make dinner, then do some stargazing?"

"That sounds like the perfect end to a perfect day." And when they finished their honeymoon, they would return to Olivia's cabin in the Florida forest where they'd decided to make their home together with Ranger.

All in all, she couldn't ask for a more perfect life.

* * * * *

If you enjoyed this story,
be sure to check out Chase's story in
Hiding The Witness
Available now from Love Inspired Suspense!

And discover more at LoveInspired.com.

Dear Reader,

Thank you so much for sharing Caleb and Olivia's story! I love flawed characters whose internal conflicts are as unique and challenging as the danger they find themselves in.

One of the things both Caleb and Olivia struggle with is the ability to trust. They've both been hurt in the past and have a difficult time learning to trust again. I think all of us go through trials in our lives that make it difficult to open up and trust one another, but as long as we continue to trust in God, I believe we can learn to trust others—and maybe even ourselves—again.

I hope you've enjoyed sharing Caleb and Olivia's journey as much as I enjoyed creating it. If you'd like to keep up with my new stories, you can find me on Facebook, Facebook.com/deenaalexanderauthor and X, X.com/deenaalexandera, or sign up for my newsletter, Gmail.us10.list-manage.com/subscribe?u=d7e6e9ecdc08 88d7324788ffc&id=42d52965df.

Deena Alexander

Harlequin® Reader Service

Enjoyed your book?

Try the perfect subscription for Romance readers and get more great books like this delivered right to your door.

See why over 10+ million readers have tried Harlequin Reader Service.

Start with a Free Welcome Collection with free books and a gift—valued over $20.

Choose any series in print or ebook. See website for details and order today:

TryReaderService.com/subscriptions